Escaping Bondage

Tiffany Moree

Tiffany Moree

To order products, or for any other correspondence:

escapingbondage@gmail.com

Book and Cover Design by:
MADD Cre8tive Studio

ISBN 9780991554102

Bel Ekri Publishing

Tiffany Moree

DEDICATED TO MY MOTHER

Tiffany Moree

TABLE OF CONTENTS

Chapter 1

I watched in horror as the two men snatched up a girl and threw her into the back of their van. I was petrified; I was witnessing a kidnapping, and I couldn't even move. I had to call someone, anyone! I rummaged through my cluttered backpack for my phone. It had to be in here, it had to be. All hope drained from me as I discovered I had left my phone under my pillow at home.

The one problem for me in this situation was I couldn't leave my hiding spot. I was hiding in some bushes that were right across from my house. The kidnappers weren't moving their van; it was like they were waiting for someone; maybe more victims.

Looking over at the van I saw one of the men getting out. His face was hidden by the dimmed streetlights and the absence of moonlight. His walk was cool, comfortable almost, like he had done this a hundred times. A lone girl, too short to be older than I, walked down the sidewalk; her

purse was clutched to her side as she strolled casually, her phone occupying her attention, unaware of the danger before her. The man ran into her, holding the cloth against her face before she could utter a peep. Her body slumped and he grabbed her in his arms, carrying her to the van and putting her inside.

It seemed like they had gotten what they needed and the tires screeched as they fled the scene. My legs were moving as fast as they could go; I'd hop the fence instead of going around mainly because my life was in danger. I crossed the street, getting half way before items began to slip from my backpack. My hands shook and the sound of my heart echoed like a low drum as I tried to pick up each item.

A bright light, blinding and unwelcoming shined on me and as the tires from a car came to a rough halt, I froze. I knew what was happening; hands covered my mouth, replaced quickly by a damp cloth, and the final sound heard was the closing of their van doors as my world shattered into a dark abyss.

There were sounds around me; heavy breathing, the same repetitive drop of water, and the sound of my own heart matching my emotions. A recollection of memories flooded in at once; it made reality seem almost unrealistic even though it was, in fact, reality.

Suddenly there was a light, not like previously, and this time with the light seemed evil instead of good. There were two men, the ones who had taken me and the other girls. As my vision adjusted, I noticed those two girls, bindings around their wrists and ankles and around their abdomens, tape covering their mouths. I looked down, seeing I too was in the same bindings.

The men were now visible, each wearing their own look. The one with dark hair stepped forward, having a sinister look of his own with no resemblance to the other man who stood back.

The darker haired man began to walk toward us circling around our chairs like a lion toying with its prey, "I take it you all realize what happened. So instead of letting you ask those . . ." he paused, his hand gently grazing the face of the girl beside me, ". . . silly little questions you're dying to ask. I'll answer them for you."

"My name is Clyde; this here is my partner, Eric." He pointed to the man with the blonde hair, young in features and decent looks but still something was off about him and it unsettled my stomach.

"Here we run an organized and extremely strict system of girls of most ages. You will be joining this system, obeying rules, following protocols, and working efficiently." The thought that came to my mind as he talked was the word *slave*. We'd have to work and serve them for some sort of profit they'd get out of it in the end. But none of us would be treated right.

"There are over two hundred girls who reside here. Like them, you will work for the one thing that everyone wants," Clyde paused.

"Freedom," Eric finished for him, taking a step forward.

"Finally, you'll be given a tracking device and security device that keeps you from escaping or walking out the front door. It's impossible to take off, so don't bother." Clyde walked back, knocking on the steel door which opened, and two girls walked in carrying a tray of clothes and tiny items.

Eric whispered something in the ear of one of the girls, his eyes briefly looking to me before he slipped her something then left with Clyde following behind.

The two girls, one older than the other, removed the tape from our mouths and the ropes that bound us.

"Can you tell us where we are?" I turned my head to the girl beside me who was speaking, yet the two females ignored her. "Please, why did they take us? Do you know a way out?" the girl continued with urgency in her voice.

I was handed clothes which matched their own; the dull grey dresses resembled nurses' uniforms from the 1960s.

"Just tell me something, anything—"

"You're wasting your time!" I yelled at her, and she looked at me. Her sweat-soaked blonde hair was sticking to her forehead as her face began to form into a solid frown. "They don't know any more than you . . . so you're wasting your time."

She put on a look of defeat, no longer bothering the two girls with her questions.

We were given the tracking devices they told us about; metal bands that stuck to our skin like handcuffs, cold and inescapable. I complied because everything at this point was inevitable. I put on the clothes and the slip-on shoes.

"I'm Helen, I am the head of the girl's here, and I will be going over a few extra rules and protocols as I take you to your rooms." The older woman instructed us to stand; she took us out of the room and into a hallway which I believed led into the center of the building.

"Here, you no longer hold on to the lives you've left behind. The quicker you let go, the easier it will be. The longer you hold on, the longer your stay in hell will seem." We had left the corridor now and were moving into the center, levels upon levels, at least six floors—different areas all compiled into one large facility resembling a prison and a high-tech bee-hive all compacted together.

"Robin, please take number one and number two to the auditorium." My arm was gripped by Helen, who stopped me while the other's walked ahead.

"Pin this to your clothes," She held out a metal pin, shaped like a familiar flower I once saw in a memory. My eyes met Helen's briefly before I pinned the flower to my dress. We walked through the building then through a pair of doors.

We stood inside a large auditorium; rows were piling up with girls in those plain matching outfits. Everything was orderly around here, yet it was like a curtain of despair over everything.

I followed behind Helen, sensing numerous eyes on the back of my head. How had this happened to me so suddenly? I was instructed up the stairs of the stage and sat in the empty chair next to one of the girls kidnapped with me. She had been crying this entire time; her nose was red and her face was puffy. I couldn't blame her or anyone for that matter; we were all going through the same shit and if I could fully take in the situation, I'd probably be reacting the same way.

The audience had become quiet and in walked Clyde and Eric. The two walked on stage and I couldn't help but notice how close Eric was; on the inside I knew what it meant, but I hoped that this wasn't the case.

"Welcome ladies," Clyde said excitedly into the microphone, facing the crowd. "Stand girls," Eric commanded us. We all stood.

"Okay Eric, you name her and I will name the other two." Clyde declared, whispering just loud enough for Eric and the rest of us to hear. They were stripping us of our names? It was unfair, they not only took us from our lives, but now our names. It wasn't right.

"You will be called…Holly," he said referring to the one with blonde hair.

"And you will be called Sarah." He added, pointing to the second girl, who'd been quiet the entire time, hiding behind her chestnut hair.

"Finally, you will be called…Sydney." I almost had to stop myself from choking. How did he…why did he name me my actual name? How does he even know my name? I was cut off by Clyde's sudden outburst.

"Welcome your new sisters Sarah, Holly, and Sydney!" Clyde yelled and the room exploded with clapping. I looked around the audience and noticed a brunette girl glaring at me. I ignored her glare and turned my attention to Eric. Maybe he isn't bad at all; he did end up letting me keep my name.

We were swiftly taken to the control room to get our bands entered into the system. Each band had our names inscribed on it.

"Choose, Clyde." Eric said as we were walking out of the control room.

"Sarah, I know I'll have some fun with her." Clyde smirked wickedly and snatched Sarah's arm. She yelped. My eyes darted between the two men. What was happening?

"Please, you don't have to—" his viscous slap to her face made her stop talking. Tears rolled down her tanned cheeks. My eyes grew wide and I expected that Holly or I would be next.

I wanted to run and hide, shield myself from the upcoming nightmare, another part of me wanted snap one of their necks then make a break for it, but either way it was inevitable.

"I'll take her; you decide what you want to do with the other two." Clyde dragged Sarah out of the hallway and into the elevator. She gave me a weak smile before the elevator doors shut.

"Holly, you're of no interest to me. Leave." He ordered her. I was shocked at how harsh he sounded.

"You," He smiled and moved toward me. I felt alarmed feeling his breath fan my face. This wasn't going to end the way I had thought, but what did I expect? Cupcakes and rainbows? He lifted his hand about to touch my cheek.

"Please—"

"Shh…don't beg, it will only make me angry." He smiled. I felt a tear roll down my cheek. He cupped my face with on hand and wiped away the tear. I instantly flinched, turning my head away from him.

"You should feel special. You're the only girl who's ever caught my eye. Don't think of it as forced. If you want, you can enjoy it." He smiled casually and it pissed me off. Why did he think I would enjoy this? It was rape! And was that why the brunette was eyeing me so strangely in the audience? Was this guy some sort of praised individual?

"Come with me." He grabbed my hand and pulled me along. I stayed quiet along the way, trying to prepare myself for all of the possibilities. He stayed on the second floor. We took the steps. I received numerous glares and glances from the other girls and it only gave me insight on how insane this place actually was.

We reached what I assumed was his room. It was large, with a dark colors as a sort of theme, it matched his hidden personality, one that was twisted and frightening.

He then removed his shirt and I felt my stomach turn inside out.

"Come." He ordered me. I hesitated, only slightly but he noticed and his eyes narrowed; almost instantly I stood, walking towards him slowly, hoping to avoid this situation for as long as possible. He pulled my arm, yanking me forward and spun me around so my back was facing him. He unzipped my dress and began kissing my lower back. I wasn't sure how I was supposed to feel, but it fell in between the lines of pleasure and displeasure; numb.

"Does that feel good?" He asked as his lips trailed up my back.

"Yes." It's what he wanted to here, right? It'd keep me alive and I'd see tomorrow, but I didn't want this...I needed to try and get away.

He slipped off the dress and it fell to the floor, leaving me in my underwear. I tried to hold back my tears. I wanted my first time to be with my husband...not my kidnapper. This was so screwed up.

He held my hips then pulled me close to him, so my back was touching his chest. His lips touched my shoulder, and then he began to nibble on my skin. I whimpered quietly, but he heard it.

Chapter 2

His hands stopped roaming and suddenly he shoved me roughly onto the bed.

He brought his body on top of mine and leaned down, barely hovering over my lips, so close I could smell his minty breath and hear the sound of him swallowing hard.

I shut my eyes, sucking in one final breath before I felt him lift himself from off me.

"Go," he commanded me.

"What?" I questioned, stupidly. This means I can leave, pure and free, I should be out the door by now.

"I've had enough fun for tonight, go." I sat up and got off the bed, slipping my clothes on quickly before leaving.

The women I met when I first got here met me at the bottom of the steps.

"I'm going to take you to your room, which is on the third floor." She smiled. Why do I have to be so close to Eric's floor? I wish I was on the eighth floor or at least the fourth.

"What's your name again?" I asked her. I'm terrible at remembering names, and really I hoped that I wasn't here long enough to remember.

"Helen." She gave me a small smile and led me to the elevator.

We reached the third floor in a matter of seconds. She walked in front of me, guiding me to my new room.

"Room three-twenty; you will be sharing this room with…" She trailed off and looked down at her clipboard.

"Jane. She's a quiet one, so you won't have any trouble with her. The lights go out at 10:30. And breakfast is served at nine, lunch is at one in the afternoon, and finally dinner is served at seven. If you miss dinner, you can't have anything else to eat and a guaranteed shock from your band." Everything was so orderly; it was kind of a shock.

"Oh! Being on time earns you a point at each meal. And if you didn't know, points are earned for each deed you accomplish, and every five hundred points gives you another name in the bucket for the drawing at the end of the year. Have a good night, Sydney." She smiled, and then walked down the hall, attending to other duties. I'm guessing she's a very important person. She looked older than most of the girls I've seen here.

She might've been here the longest. At least she attempts to be happy. I mean this place seemed luxurious except for the fact that we're all prisoners.

I opened the door to my new room slowly. I walked inside. The room was all white, matching the building. On either side were twin beds and a night stand with lamps placed on top. Everything was clean, not a speck of dust anywhere.

A girl with a tiny frame sat on her bed reading a novel. She didn't acknowledge my presence nor did she even care that I was here. She was probably shy, and if she wanted to talk, she would. So it was best if I left her alone.

I walked to my bed and sat down. It was a springy mattress, which I hated. I guess it'll have to do… until I leave this place.

I looked out the window which separated me from my freedom. I guess suicide wasn't an option either. I sighed. If it meant serving Clyde and Eric to the fullest extent to leave this place, then I'd do it. I wasn't going to be here for very long. I was leaving early. My family…they'd miss me. They probably already know I've gone missing. I hope they're searching.

"Lights out!" I heard someone yell. I knew it was night time, but I didn't think it was that late. Jane had already flipped off her light, even before they told us to. I was curious about her. Maybe she was quiet for a reason. I sighed and turned off my lamp, slipping under my warm covers and falling asleep.

I woke up around 8:30 according to the clock in the hallway. It was practically nailed to the wall. I'm guessing they didn't like weapons either. I walked downstairs and headed to the dining hall. Many girls had gotten there early like me. No one would want to be late and risk getting in trouble.

As I looked around for a seat, I spotted Sarah. Thank goodness. I didn't want to sit alone, because many of these girls had already made whatever friends they could in this place. I walked over to her. She looked like she was looking for a seat too. But the closer I got to her, the more her bruised face came into view. I wanted to run up and hug her with all my might, but I didn't know how to comfort a victim of rape. I waved and smiled as I came up to her.

"Hey Sydney! I was looking for you. I was so scared that I'd sit alone. It's like freshman year all over again." she beamed. She actually seemed alright, even though her innocence had been stolen from her.
"Let's find a table." I told her. She suddenly looped her arm through mine and we started skipping around the dining hall, looking like idiots. It probably wasn't the best idea to draw

attention to myself, because I noticed a lot of girls had been giving me dirty looks lately.

"I wouldn't be parading your screwed up face around the whole cafeteria, Sarah. It might spoil someone's appetite." Sarah stopped, and I did too.

We both looked over to the girl who made the rude comment. She was the same brunette who was glaring at me in the auditorium. Now that I had a better look of her face, she had a snooty look to her. She had long straight brunette hair and had a beautiful, arrogant-like face. She reminded me of a younger Megan Fox.

"How old are you? Ten? Because comments like that just prove how immature you are." Sarah replied, adding a small smirk at the end of her sentence.

"Want some ice for that burn?" I laughed. A few girls around us, joined in on my laughter. The brunette scowled then turns back to her friends. I really hate bullies.

We headed to a less crowded table and sat down. I looked around the table and spotted Holly. Our eyes met for a moment before she stood up and left the table. What's wrong with her?

I started chatting with Sarah before the room went immediately silent. Me and Sarah stopped talking and jumped on the bandwagon. Clyde and Eric walked up to the small square table in the front of the cafeteria and sat down.

"Good morning girls." Eric chimed.

"Good morning Eric." Everyone chorused. Sarah and I looked at each other and giggled. They sounded like robots.

"Good morning little sluts." Clyde grumbled and put his head in his hands.

"Good morning Cly-"

"Oh shut up." He groaned.

"He was drunk last night, so I'm guessing he has a hangover." Sarah whispered to me. I nodded.

"Serve the damned food already!" Clyde pounded his fist on the table and the whole room jumped. Girls wearing aprons over their dresses came out serving plates of delicious-looking food. I licked my lips hungrily. Someone set our food down in front of us and me and Sarah were about to dig in when someone snapped their fingers.
We looked at the girl across from us and she shook her head.

"You have to wait until Clyde is finished. He will decide if we get to eat or not," she informed us quietly. I nodded along with Sarah.

"I'm Robin." She extended her small hand and I shook it, then Sarah did, too. I remembered her, from the night we came here she was the girl helping Helen.

"You two are Sydney and Sarah, right?" We both nodded.

"Ok cool." She stopped talking, and then focused her attention to a strand of her curly brown hair. She had it styled in a bob which framed her slim face perfectly. She had a button nose and big hazel eyes; she reminded me of a kitten.

My stomach growled loudly, drawing everyone's attention at our table. I blushed embarrassed and held my arm over my stomach. I hadn't eaten for over a day.

"Do you think they deserve food today Clyde?" Eric spoke loud enough so all of us could hear.

"Hell no." Clyde spat and pushed himself away from the table and left the room.

"Clean this mess up and tend to your morning duties," Eric ordered us and followed Clyde out. I wanted to cry. I was being deprived of food! My

27

source of joy and happiness three times a day. This was not going to sit well with my stomach. Soon girls started getting up and leaving the dining hall.

"That drunken bastard, he does this all the time when he has a hangover." Robin complained.

"Fooooooooooddd." I drawled then whimpered, clenching my hungry stomach.

"Its fine guys. Just forget about it. By the way, Robin, what are we supposed to do?" Sarah asked.

"Each day they put up our daily chores on a bulletin board. Whichever floor you stay on is the place where you find your schedule. "She told us. "I'll see you guys later, if we're caught standing around by one of the patrols, we'll get shocked." Robin skipped off to the elevator, and Sarah disappeared. I might as well take the stairs. I climbed the two flights then came up to the bulletin board, which was crowded. I decided to wait a while for some of the girls to disperse. I walked up to the board and searched for my name.

Sydney E. was the only Sydney up there. What does "E" stand for though? My last name was Crow.

"Excuse me, what does E stand for?" I asked a girl who stood beside me.

28

"Oh my gosh! No way! No freaking way! How did you get Eric?" She screeched. Everyone's heads turned. Girls rushed towards me all asking the same questions.

"Why did you get Eric?"

"Are you his favorite?"

"How did you get him and not Clyde like everyone else?"

Everyone seemed angry so I slipped away and shut myself inside my room for a minute or two. It was true. I was his favorite, his *only* favorite. He chose me out of all of the much prettier girls who stayed here. Why did it have to be me?

I checked if the coast was clear and walked back over to the bulletin board. I noticed that my schedule was no longer stapled to the bulletin board, but thrown on the ground, crumbled with footprints on it. I uncurled it and looked over the paper.

Sydney E.

Total points: 50

Assigned permanently to: Eric

Morning chores: Report to Eric's room at 10:00 a.m.

Afternoon chores: Report to Eric's room at 2:00 p.m.

Evening chores: Report to Eric's room at 8:30 p.m.

I stood in shock reading the paper. This was all I had to do? I would much rather clean or cook like the other girls than report to Eric's stupid room! What was he going to do to me? He did say that it wouldn't be my last time going to his room. Now

he's scheduled me to spend every moment of today with him. And how did I get 50 points?! I didn't even do anything but show up on time. I glanced up at the clock and saw that it was 9:58. Crap.

I ran down the flight of stairs and tried to remember Eric's room number. I hadn't even paid attention to it! I groaned. That was when I saw Eric leaning against the wall. I dashed toward him. It was right on time too, because the clock had just struck 10.

"Good girl, I didn't think you'd remember my room so I stood out here. Come inside now." He grabbed my hand and pulled me into his room. The nervous feeling I had was coming back. I felt like I was going to throw up any food left in my stomach.

"Don't worry, Sydney; I'm not going to touch you...today. I just thought you could exercise with me." I put on a confused look. Exercise? Really? This is what he decided to do with me?

But by the lustful look in his eyes I could tell he just wanted to watch me stretch and do jumping jacks like a stupid pervert.

He went to his closet and took out a workout outfit, which consisted of tight elastic shorts and a sports bra. Perfect, just perfect. I sighed and took the outfit from him. It didn't help that he stared at me the whole time I was changing.

"Do you work out regularly? You are quite toned," he smirked. I didn't want to tell him anything about me or my past, I just wanted to get this over with.

"Yeah," I mumbled.

"Were you into any kind of sports or training programs?" His questions were annoying as hell.

"I was a cheerleader for a while," I admitted. It's only one little thing, it's not important.

"That's hot. Ok, so first let's stretch." He suddenly removed his shirt, and I averted my eyes to something else. He then went over to his stereo and turned on some music. It was some R&B song that I couldn't quite remember the name of, but it was incredibly inappropriate, but that was most likely Eric's style; inappropriate.

"Stretch over to the left and touch your foot then to the right." I did what he said, ignoring the fact that my butt was all he was focused on and he wasn't even stretching.

"Now let's bend over and touch our toes then reach up to the sky." I reluctantly followed his instructions.

The next two hours passed by with lots of stretching, jumping jacks, pushups and sit ups.

I collided with Eric's bed and gulped down all the water from my water bottle. Eric sat down beside me and drank a sip of his water. He wasn't nearly as sweaty as I was which pissed me off. He only did like half of the exercises and spent the rest of the time watching me with perverted eyes.

"You're a pervert, you know that?" I said without thinking. I immediately covered my mouth with my hands. He got up and stood in front of me.

"Am I really?" He smirked, with an evil glint in his eye.

"I'm sorry, I didn't mean to-"

"Yeah, you did. Don't take it back on account of my feelings. Just know that I'm heavily attracted to you right now, that I don't care what you say." I sat up and backed myself away from him on the bed.

"Stop moving away from me." He ordered. I did what I was told, which made me even more scared.

"I thought you said you wouldn't touch me…" I whispered.

"Yup, I did say that, and now I take it back." He grabbed my ankles and pulled me toward him. I whimpered quietly. He gripped my waist and forced his lips onto mind. I struggled slightly

under his strong grip. He was hurting my waist. I didn't respond…I couldn't, I didn't want to.

"Respond or I'll take your virginity right here, right now," he threatened. I slowly began to kiss him back, but only moving my lips against his. He suddenly gripped my face tightly and pushed me away from him.

"You can try and make me not like you, but it won't work. And if it does, then I'll make your life hell and guarantee that you won't make it out of here," he growled.

"Now, I don't care what you think of me as. But it won't be as your kidnapper or rapist. Because that's not who I will be thought of. You will develop some sort of attraction to me, and I'll make your life simpler around here. If you disobey me, you'll face the consequences. I'm trying to be patient with you. Don't make me regret choosing you Sydney. Or I might just take away your name and your life." I felt myself becoming smaller and smaller. He could do anything he wanted to, and there's nothing that could stop him. How did he even know my name?

"I looked up your file. You shouldn't say your thoughts out loud; it's not lady-like. Do I make myself clear?"

"Yes." I put my head down and felt a few tears escaping my strong hold.

"Good. Now, get dressed and leave. Lunch is about to be served," he told me. I quickly slipped my clothes back on and went back downstairs and into the dining hall.

Clyde's mood lightened up and he let us eat lunch, which was great. It turns out that after lunch we got an hour of free time, which I couldn't enjoy fully because I had to go up to Eric's room later.

"You're assigned to whom?" Robin yelled, drawing unwanted attention to Sarah and me. "Shh! Lower your voice," I told her. "I can't believe you're assigned to Eric. It's heard that no one has been assigned to him," Robin said, well informed of the topic, while I was hardly interested. I didn't want to be known as Eric's favorite. It's already bringing me unwanted attention and half of the girls hate me. But they don't know what he's really like. I barely know what he's really like. But I know he's a perverted sociopath.

"It's not a big deal." I told Robin.

"You got the only nice guy in this building. And people have been talking about your points. You've already gotten eighty, and no one gets eighty points on their second day." Her words made me feel worse. Everyone already disliked me, and now they'll think I'm getting special treatment. I don't get girls. I mean; we were all kidnapped, shouldn't we be sticking together? I know every girl in here wants to go home but do we really have to turn on each other? It's like the Hunger Games in this hell hole.

"I'm so toasted." I sighed.

"Don't worry, we're here for you." Sarah smiled.

"Thanks guys, but I have to go. Eric's expecting me and I can't be late," I told them and headed to the stairwell. I climbed the steps and walked over to Eric's room. Why did he want me to waste my time on him? What was he planning?

The door opened a few moments later and Eric revealed himself wearing a fancy tuxedo. What were we doing this time?

"Come in," he said. I slipped past him and walked over to sit down on his bed. And not to my surprise a red dress was laid down on the bed with a matching pair of red strappy heels on the floor.

"What is this about Eric?" I growled.

"Well every year we host an annual talent show. The girl who wins earns one hundred points. So, since I own you, I was thinking we could do a dance number. You'll definitely win since you have an advantage." He smirked.

"What advantage?"

"I'm a judge." He smiled. I gaped for a moment or two. He's so unfair! Why can't he just let me do this on my own? Actually, I don't want to do this at all. It's unfair to the other girls, and as long as he gives me a good grade, I'll get the 100 points. Then, every single girl in the facility will be after me. I don't want that.

"No." I protested.

"Excuse me? Did you just say *no* to me?" His eyes had a dark gleam to them, and it scared me out of my wits.

"I said no. I'm not going to cheat. It's not fair to the other girls." I told him.
"You're so innocent," he spat. And I could feel the hatred coming from the word "innocent."

"I'm sorry-"

"Nope, it's definitely too late for that. He yanks my arm and drags me out of the room. Fear is spread across my face. What is he doing? People were looking at us and whispering.

He dragged me into the elevator but didn't press any buttons.

"You are really bad at listening!" he yelled. He probably chose the elevator so no one would hear him yelling at me.

"If I tell you to do something, that's what you'll do! I'm a nice guy, but you're starting to become rebellious!" he shouted. I winced and maneuvered myself into the corner of the elevator. He roughly pressed floor number eight and started pacing back and forth. When the elevator opened he grabbed my arm again. He pulled me toward the railing and took out a key. He quickly unlocked the band on my wrist, and then gripped the back of my neck and pushed it down over the railing.

"Give me one good reason why I shouldn't let you plummet to your death!" He yelled. I heard gasps coming from bystanders who were watching him and me.

"I'll do anything y-you say! I promise! Please don't kill me! I'm begging you!" I sobbed loudly. "What else?"

"I'll do whatever you like, and I'll be in the talent show. I won't argue! I promise!" I looked down below; the drop was at least an 80 foot drop to hard marble floors.

"Now apologize!" he hissed.

"I'm sorry! I'm so sorry Eric. I'm sorry," I cried. He released my neck and I fell on the floor.

"Meet me back at my room." He mumbled as he left me sobbing on the ground. I hated him. I hated him with a burning passion. I was tired of being treated like this. I needed to find some way out.

Chapter 3

"Okay, so let's sort this all out. Sydney seduces Eric, thus slipping the key from his pocket. She wins the talent show. And afterwards, comes to get us to take our wristbands off. Then, we head to the control room and open the front doors. We get out and then we run for our lives. How did you come up with this?" Sarah asks me.

"When Eric tried to throw me over the rail, he took the key right out of his pocket and took off my band. As I thought about it I remembered that suicide is prohibited. So like if you tried to jump, the band would shock you. And if we tried to escape, our bands would shock us in the process. By taking them off, we can leave freely." I explained to them.

"Are you sure this will work?" Robin asked.

"I'm hoping it will. I don't even know how to seduce someone, but I guess it's worth it. But if we get caught, it can end badly." I told them.

"Let's do it." Sarah smirked and we all joined hands and then threw them up in the air.

~~~~

Step One: Seduce Eric

39

I informed Eric that I was going to meet him before the show. He had agreed smoothly.

I walked into his dimmed room. There were candles everywhere. What the hell?

"Sorry about the dark room, the lights aren't working." He appeared in front of me holding a candle. He was such a bad liar; the lights in the hallway were working perfectly fine.

"So, why did you want to meet before the show?" he asked.

"I thought we could go over the dance again," I told him.

"Ok." He placed the candle on his dresser and we got in our positions. The music started and we began. I had decided that when the one slow and steady part of the song came on, I could make my move.

Step Two: Take the Keys

Instead of doing the dip like I was supposed to, I wrapped one of my legs around his leg. He stared at me in amusement. I slung my arms around his neck and brought myself closer to him. He leaned down and started kissing my neck. I took this opportunity to silently slip the key out of his pocket.

"I could take you right now. But we have a talent show to do," he whispered in my ear, making me feel nothing but disgust. He patted my butt and then left the room. I smiled and dangled the key in front of my face. Home, here I come.

I hid the key in my bra, where it wouldn't be found. The auditorium was packed full of people. Everyone was required to attend the talent show, even though not everyone had to participate. I made my way to my seat next to Robin and Sarah.

"I've got it." I whispered.

"Yes! We'll be home in no time." Robin said in a hushed tone. We sat back in our seats and I could feel excitement radiating from them. Unlike them, I was worried. What if we got caught? What if someone saw us leaving and decided to tell Clyde and Eric to get extra points? Not only could I get in trouble but I'm also responsible for Robin and Sarah. Clyde is ruthless and won't hold back like Eric. And Eric…who knows what he'll do to me.

The talent show began and plenty acts followed, but sooner than I had wished, we were up next.

"Next up we have Sydney performing a dance with none other than Eric," the girl on the stage announced. The audience clapped as I walked on to the stage with Eric by my side. I could tell that everyone was pissed at me because there was no doubt that I was going to win, which ultimately sucked.

"Ready?" Eric whispered to me.

"Ready." I nodded.

The upbeat Latin music played and our bodies went into motion. We swayed rhythmically to the music, doing occasional spins and turns. Our bodies moved together perfectly and I'm sure everyone was interested. Eric didn't look at me during the dance like we had practiced, but I guess he was as nervous as I was.

Our dance ended with Eric dipping me in a sexy sort of way. The audience applauded and we exited the stage.

I went back to my seat as the last performer went on. It was two girls singing to a Justin Timberlake song in an off-tone key. It sounded like someone strangling a pregnant cat on a highway. It was terrible. And Clyde looked like he was going to pop a blood vessel by the way he clenched his fists.

"You tone death whores! Get off the damn stage! You both sound like dying birds!" Clyde hollered at them. The girl's scurried off the stage and went back to their seats. Clyde could be cruel, but he was right about their singing.

"And now to announce the winners of the talent show!" Helen came onto the stage holding an envelope.

"In third place winning 30 points is…Becky!" The girl named Becky ran onto the stage and gave everyone her gap-toothed smile. She had done ballet for her talent. It was a snooze-fest.

"In second place winning 50 points is . . . Courtney!" Helen announced. I had finally known the name of the brunette bimbo who envied me. She walked up to the stage and flashed a perfect smile. I had missed her performance because I went to the bathroom at the time. My bladder is more important than Courtney.

"And in first place winning 100 points is . . . Sydney!" No one applauded, which wasn't a shock to me. Only Robin and Sarah whooped and hollered. I gave the audience a small smile before we were told to get off stage again.

Robin, Sarah, and I, had slipped away before they dismissed us; it'd give us time to leave before getting caught. We had slipped out of the auditorium and went to the control room. We unlocked the front doors and took off our bands. Freedom was seconds away.
Step Three: Leave This Shit-hole!

"We're getting out of here girls. This is fantastic!" Sarah cheered.

"I'm a smart man, you know that Sydney?" A voice erupted from the door and Eric and Clyde came walking in.

"And a smart man knows when something is missing. You're the only one that I was around in the last hour. I figured it out the moment I noticed it right before we got on stage, because I always like to make sure I have my key on me at all times." He smirked. This can't be happening. We were supposed to get away safe and sound! But we never even had a glimpse of freedom.

"Eric I'm so—"

"Sorry? Yeah, you're only sorry because you got caught in the act. But after I'm through with you, you're going to wish that you were sorry." he snarled. I could feel the tension rising in the room. I caught glimpses of Robin's and Sarah's faces. They were horrified. This was all my fault.

"Auditorium. *Now.*" Clyde ordered us.

The auditorium was still packed full of girls and I had a really bad feeling about this. They were going to do something crazy in front of everyone. "Attention girls. As you see; these three little trouble makers were trying to escape a few minutes ago. Now we've never had anyone try to escape before, so let me teach you all a little lesson about breaking the rules," Clyde spoke into the microphone. He hesitated for a moment and then removed a gun from his pocket.

"Poor little Robin, you were such an obedient girl. What a waste." He pointed the gun at her. "Clyde please!" I screamed before I was cut off by the firing of the gun. I fell to my knees my eyes spilling out countless tears. I glanced over to Sarah, her face was like a stone statue.

"Sarah...you were such a good toy until you were corrupted by this whore. So you can blame her for your death." Clyde cocked the gun and pulled the trigger ending another innocent life. I felt my heart shattering inside of me. I couldn't breathe and my head was pounding.

"See what you did? It's your fault their dead Sydney! Not mine!" Clyde shouted at me and tossed the gun down. Eric had just stood by watching the events take place with a sour expression on his face.

"Everyone go to your rooms!" Clyde yelled. The girls dispersed in a matter of seconds.

This was a dream. Just a terrible dream. I couldn't get their lifeless bodies out of my head. It was my fault. I should have acted alone. Then it'd be me instead of them. There was a huge lump in my throat that I couldn't swallow.

It was guilt.

"Meet me in my room in five minutes," Eric sighed as he left me on the stage to mourn for my friends.

I rose to my feet and grabbed the gun from the stage. I checked to see if any bullets were left. There were two. I ran out of the auditorium and went up to my room first. Jane was sleeping soundly in her bed as I hid the gun under my pillow.

I slipped back out of my room and headed downstairs to Eric's. As I went down each step, the pain in my chest grew worse. Something bad was going to happen. And I had the best guess on what it was.

I knocked lightly on Eric's door, which he immediately opened. He opened the door wide so I could slip past him. I went over to the bed and sat down.

"You brought this upon yourself. You could have stayed a virgin, Sydney. I wasn't even thinking about raping you until now. I put my trust in you. But, you better hope I don't enjoy this, because if I do, you're in for a lot of pain." I gulped back my tears. Knowing that I was about to be violated in the most horrific way was something I couldn't deal with. I had to find some way to not think about it, to make my mind go numb or blank.

"And to make sure you stay awake," he revealed a small pocket knife.

"Eric, please!" I cried out. He snatched me up by my hair, and then pinned me down. He gripped my thigh tightly and pressed the blade against my skin.

"This is going to hurt." He said before jabbing the knife in my thigh. A high-pitched scream erupted from me. I could feel the blood seeping out of my fresh wound. The pain was unimaginable. I couldn't stop the tears from escaping my eyes.

Eric violently ripped away my dress along with any remaining clothing. I was frozen the entire time. Everything else that happened was a blur, one big blur blinded by tears and the throbbing pain from my thigh, then everything slowly went dark.

"Good morning girls." Eric sang, to the clueless females.

"Good morning Eric." Everyone repeated. I, on the other hand was lost in space. I was sore between my legs and my body was bruised and battered from the events from last night.

Apparently, Eric was frustrated that I had passed out, so he said he'd do it again tonight. He was sick. Why did I have to belong to him? I was his one and only victim, so I never got a break.

And he said he'd start giving me points again when he was sure that I was a "good girl."

"Good morning, bitches." Clyde snorted.

"Good morning, Clyde." They all replied.

"Now, girls, I have a project for you all. But I will announce it after breakfast." Eric said. Project? What, another way to earn points?

We all ate breakfast in silence after Clyde had finished. I had no one to talk to…since Robin and Sarah. I felt a few tears pecking at my cheeks but I wiped them away without a second thought.

"Okay girls, today we are playing hide and seek." Everyone froze. Hide and seek?

"The seekers are all of you, and the hider is none other than the wonderful Sydney." Eric simpered, looking satisfied with my reaction. No, no, no! Why is he doing this? It's not just a game; I can tell it's more than that.
"Now, whoever brings Sydney back to me or Clyde, wins five hundred points." My stomach

turned. Everyone was going to be after me. I had to find some place to hide.

"You all know the rules; you must find the hider and bring her back in twenty minutes, or she gets the five hundred points. If you break anything you will be shocked, and finally you can hurt the hider to get her to comply. Sydney," Eric looked over at me.

"You have five minutes to hide." He grinned. Everyone was staring at me like I was the last piece of meat. I was utterly terrified, but I wasn't going to lose this game.
"And…go!" I jumped up from my seat and ran for the elevator. Helen had given me some pain killers for my thigh and stitched up my wound, but I could still feel the slight throbbing from where Eric harmed me.

I could hide in the girl's bathroom on the seventh floor. I know a small vent in there that I could probably fit into. I sped out the elevator and ran to the bathroom. I slid on my knees and up to the small vent.

It took me a while to get the cover off and then into the vent again while holding the covering in place. I had a watch on me so I could tell when the game was over.

Outside the bathroom I heard girls yelling and footsteps passing by. I glanced at my watch in the lights shining through the vents.

Seventeen minutes left to go. I should stick to hiding here. No one would dare expect me to climb into a vent.

"That slut is a great hider. No one's found her yet. Gosh, I hate her so much. Why does Eric like her so much?" Voices entered the bathroom, and searched the stalls. I wanted to laugh. Girls can get so jealous. Do they not realize that Eric is a damn rapist? He's cruel and ruthless. And they're jealous of me. I would rather deal with Clyde.

"Eric must be lonely. He probably chose her because she bribed him somehow." Another one assumed. Bribed him? With what? My virginity? Ha-ha, freaking ha! I wish they'd leave.

"Anyways, let's go find her." They left the bathroom and went into the hallway. At least they won't come back.

I held my watch up to the light in the vent. There was about 15 minutes left. Some people could be so clueless.

"Hey Sydney." Someone spoke. What? I looked through the vent and saw Jane staring straight at me. No…how did she?

"You know, someone's going to find you eventually. Not every girl in this place is stupid," she informed me.

"You're not turning me in?" I asked.

"I was thinking about it, but I've already gotten my five hundred points. I just thought I'd try and find you just for fun." She smiled.

"Is that why you're so laid back?"

"I guess so. I'm quite happy to know that every extra point I get is another name in the drawing. I'm ahead of most girls, so I just stick to the basic stuff," she explained.

"But five hundred points could give you five hundred more chances. Why not?"

"But that doesn't necessarily mean my name will be drawn. And plus, you've been through a lot. I don't think you need any more suffering-" she yelped as she held onto her band.

"Looks like I've said too much. Goodbye, Sydne-"

"You found Sydney, where is she Jane?!" A group of girls came through the door.

"No . . . I was talking to myself. I was preparing myself to find her that's all." She muttered quietly.

The lead girl stepped forward, shoving Jane back a little and making her stumble.

"Where is she? I need those 500 points. I'm getting out of here," the lead girl spat.

"I don't know." Jane was nice for covering for me, but she was such a bad liar. I wasn't just going to sit here and watch her get pushed around. Screw Eric and screw this game.

My hands pushed the vent door out and it landed with a clank. The girls turned to me.

"I knew she was lying." The leader said while pushing Jane to the side.

"Hey leave her alone!" I slid out of the vent and was heading toward Jane, but the girl had grabbed my arm.

"Oh, no you don't. You're coming with us," she hissed. I didn't take too kindly to girls who put their hands on me, and she wasn't an exception. I yanked my arm back and walked over to Jane. This was going to become a fight, I could already tell.

"Are you alright Jane?" She nodded and gave me a weak smile.

"Sydney come here!" My arms were pulled and my body flung into a wall.

"You stupid cunt!" I spun around and tackled the girl. The next few minutes were a blur. There was grabbing and tugging, someone's blood was on my shirt. It could have been mine. Jane had been screaming something and then I started being hauled away by a group of girls.

"Let me go!" I yelled.

"How much time do we have?" someone asked.

"Thirty seconds." Everyone groaned and dropped me to the ground.

"You stupid ass, it's your fault." I scoffed and rolled over on my stomach to push myself off the ground.

"It's everyone's fault…for not acting like human beings!" I yelled so everyone could hear me. These girls were brainwashed and deluded. They had forgotten their humanity was, and were working mindlessly. I hope to never be like them.

Tiffany Moree

Chapter 4

Clap, clap, clap, clap, clap.

Eric applauded me slowly as I came up to him. Everyone had crowded around seeing what would happen next.

"I didn't think you could do it. Boy was I wrong. You know Sydney; you've always had that fight in you, that strength coming from deep within. It's what caused you to resist me, to talk back, and to try to escape. Even after I stole something precious of yours, you still keep fighting." I didn't know where he was going with this, but nothing good was coming out of it.

"So, Sydney, I'm going to give you a little test, actually, a series of tests. And I'll, and everyone else, will see how long you last before you're broken. The tests will begin when you least expect them, and that's how I'll get you." A devious smirk spread across his face. Anger seeped inside of me. He wanted to break my confidence and my hope. He wanted me to end up like the others. They all probably gave up too quickly, and because I'm the only one seen as a threat, he comes after me.

"Alright, back to your chores girls." Eric announced and came towards me.

"Come with me." At first I had thought we were headed for Eric's room, but we went inside the control room.

"Why are we in here?" I asked.

"I want you to meet the technician. His name is Luke. He's about your age." He led me through a door and into a room filled with buttons. Someone was sitting in a chair, and the chair spun around and revealed the technician. And of course he was attractive, just like Eric. What is this? Pretty boy club?

"Um, hi . . . I'm Luke." he shook my hand once then sat back down.

"He's also my younger brother." Eric said and instantly Luke became my enemy, not that he already wasn't, but now he's not going to see the kind side of me. He's Eric's younger brother and the technician to this hell-hole. He runs the system, and judging by the cameras, he tends to spy on everyone.

"Why are we here?" I snapped, not caring how I sounded.

"You'll be spending plenty of time with me, but of course I'm sure that gets boring, so I decided to let you hang out with Luke for the remainder of the time. Have fun." Before I could object, Eric left. Damn him and his brother. I hate this place.

"So…"

"Screw you." I scoffed and sat down in a nearby chair.

"Nice to meet you too." He sighed and went back to his nerd duties.

For about an hour we both just sat; off in our own little worlds. And all I could think about was my family.

We consisted of four children, including me. My sister Madeline was the youngest. She had recently turned 7 years old. We threw her one big birthday bash with balloon animals and clowns, although the clowns were a bit creepy. She smiled a lot. It was cute when she smiled because her two front teeth were missing.

I'm a middle child, along with my twin brother, Scott. We are very similar around the face, but he's much taller and has a nice jawline. He's older than me by three minutes. His eyes are a deep shade of blue, while mine are pretty plain. People always took a liking to Scott, he was more outgoing than me and people thought of me as an standoffish, rather than someone they'd like to spend time with.

The oldest of us all is my brother Blake who is 21 and married to a woman called Vanessa, and they have a daughter on the way. We never talked much, but he's still cool.

Before I was kidnapped, my parents were in the process of a divorce. They said they didn't get along as well as they used to and thought it was best if they split for now and stay friends until things were situated between them. Personally I never cared. Shit happens. I had school to worry about…well I used to have school to worry about, now it's just being abused, raped, and chased around this prison.

I miss them all so much. Even though we weren't perfect, we all still loved each other and spent time together whenever the time came. I can't imagine what's going through their minds right now. They're probably on edge, panicked, stressed out and worried sick about me. If only they knew I was still healthy and alive.

Scott's POV

"She texted me saying that she was on her way home." My mother sobbed as she spoke to the police officer. Three things were going through my head; she was either with a friend, kidnapped, or something worse.

"Scott!" I whipped my head around to look at my father.

"Yes?" I say snapping back into reality.

"When was the last time you saw your sister?" The cop questioned.
"At the end of the school day, she was walking with her best friend Lisa, and I'm pretty sure she went to her house." The cop nodded and scribbled everything down in a little notepad.

"So can you find her?" I ask. Every ounce of hope was illuminating from me. She had to be okay. She wasn't dead. If she was dead, then I'd feel it, right? We were twins, and that had to mean something.

"Of course, son; we'll get back to you in two weeks time and give you any information we've picked up. Have a goodnight folks," the cop said and turned around to head out the door.

"Two weeks? They expect us to just sit back and wait for two weeks so they can drag her body bag in here and tell us they failed?" Blake exclaimed as his wife clutched his arm.

"Blake, lower your voice. Your mother doesn't need any more stress right now. I think it's best if we all head upstairs and get some sleep," Dad said as he walked him and Mom up the steps. Blake stormed out of the house with Vanessa running after him.

I looked down at Maddie whose face was red.

"Come on Maddie. I'm sure she'll be home soon," I told her and patted her on the back. She shrugged off my hand and ran upstairs.

Sydney, please be alright.

~~~~

Sydney's POV

My body lay naked underneath the white sheets of Eric's bed. He had left a few minutes ago, leaving me here without my clothes, which he took with him.

He was pure evil. That nice guy that I saw the first day was just a sham to get me to trust him. But now I know what kind of monster he is.

"Eric, I have those documents you—" Luke came into the room but stopped when he saw the position I was currently in.

"Crap, that prick tricked me," he swore.

"Well can you leave?" That's when a sharp pain shot through my wrist and I figured that meant that Eric wanted Luke to stay.

"Shocked?"

"Yeah," I replied.

"Listen, I'm not like my brother, he's--" he starts to talk, but I cut him off.

"I don't care what you're like. I don't trust you nor him, so don't try and be all buddy-buddy with me so you can manipulate me," I spat at him, venom spilling from my harsh tone.

"So are you two together?" he asked, brushing off my rude remark.

"Hell no, he took advantage of me…not like it's any of your business anyways." I scoffed.

"Wait what?! You're lying, he would never rape someone," he tells me.

"I'm pretty sure he has. He seems quite experienced with raping girls," I reply sarcastically.

"That sick bastard," he mutters.

"Don't act all innocent Luke, you've probably stole some innocent girl's virginity too," I spat.

"You really think that I'm that sick and perverted, that I'd rape some girl? Only weak men do that," he said.

"And you're not a weak man?"

"No, I'm a real man. Real men have wives or girlfriends and treat them with respect." he said.

"Wow, you really are a wimp, just like Eric said," I taunt, tugging at his nerves. Eric never actually said that, but I was just in a bad mood.

"And you really are a slut, just like Eric said," he retorts, glaring at me.

"I'm not a slut!" I scream and throw a pillow at him.

"And I'm not a wimp." He yells.

"Get out!" I ordered him and pointed towards the door. He storms out, not bothering to say anything else. Stupid asshole. I'm no slut, and I never will be.

Eric returns minutes later, pissed that I let Luke leave. Eric wanted me to sleep with him for some strange perverted reason. And because I didn't, I've added another bruise to my collection.

~~~~

The next morning was terrible. One of the girls was found dead in her room. She had somehow gotten a knife from the kitchen and slit her throat. And before her other friend could slit her throat, the band shocked her and she dropped the knife.

Clyde was beyond angry. He didn't understand why no one saw her go into the kitchen and steal the knife. He took it out on us by depriving us of our breakfast and lunch, but when I went up to see Eric, he gave me food, which was nice of him, but I still hate him.

Jane and I have recently started talking more. After that incident with hide and seek, we've become a bit closer. Although, she's still distant like always.

I walked up the steps, heading to my room. There was a long wait at the elevators, and I needed the exercise. I opened the door to my room and saw Jane sitting on her bed holding something small and black. Her face looked shocked and she was frozen in place. The pistol from the night Robin and Sarah were killed.

"Jane I--"

"Where did you get this?" She asked.

"The auditorium when Clyde shot…them." I told her.

"We could kill them. You could kill Eric. I could kill Clyde. We could escape!" She spoke with tears rolling down her cheeks as she looked up at me with hope in her eyes.

"No!" I yelled and snatched the gun away from her and slipped it back under my pillow.

"What do you mean *no*? We can escape! All of us," she said, giving me a confused look.

"No, I'm not going through that again. I've tried escaping once and I got two girls killed! Imagine if the plan went wrong, and you got killed, or anyone else involved was killed. I'm not going to be responsible for anyone's death. I won't have any more blood on my hands!" I yelled.

"If it goes wrong, it goes wrong, at least we tried," she whispers.

"It won't go wrong, because I'm turning this gun in and no one is killing anyone," I told her and grabbed the gun and headed for the door.

"You're going to regret this. I know what secrets they hide. This place isn't good Sydney. We can't stay here," she whimpers.

"See you later, Jane." I leave the room and head to Eric's.

"Happy Abortion Day!" Eric yells as girls file into the nurse's office. Abortion Day?

"What the hell is Abortion Day?" I ask a girl near me.

"You take a test. If you're pregnant, you get it aborted. Clyde hates babies and doesn't like wearing protection," she whispers to me.

"Everyone take a test and head to the stalls, and return with your test in ten minutes." Helen had said this. I assume she's one of the nurses. I haven't seen her in weeks, yet she looks no different than she did before. Her hair is dull, her eyes are lifeless and she never smiles, except when it's forced.

Everyone took a test and went to the bathroom. Had Eric ever used protection? I don't think he has since he's too horny to bother putting a condom on. And that's when it hit me.

I'd missed my period. I'm two weeks late. This usually doesn't happen. I will not give up my child! She or he deserves to live his or her life. And if I get out of here, the baby will be fine. I spot Holly heading into a nearby bathroom and follow her in. I have an idea.

65

"Holly, hey!" I say as I catch up to her.

"What do you want?" she asks.

"Clyde never…touched you, right?" I ask.

"Yeah, because I'm too ugly." She frowns.

"You're not ugly! You're prettier than half the girls here. And plus Clyde is sloppy, why would you want him to?" I tell her. She smiles briefly.

"Let me guess, you want me to pee on your stick because you're pregnant and want to keep the baby?" She cocks an eyebrow at me. She's good.

"Yes, please?" I begged. She hesitates but then nods and smiles. I hand her my test and she takes it into the stall with her. It was kind of gross when you thought about it; holding a stick with someone else's pee on it.

She comes out and hands me mine. We wait for a little while and then check the test. I smile seeing the single red line.

"Thank you so much Holly, I really should have stuck with you throughout these weeks," I tell her and go in for a hug. She hugs me back and then releases me.

"No problem. But if I would have stuck with you, I would have been dead too. And no one would pee on your stick for you." She tells me. Although her comment stung a bit, she was right.

We came downstairs together and everyone put their name on their test before handing it in.

We were told to return later to finish the whole process.

"Sydney," I heard my name being called and turned around and saw Eric.

"Yes?"

"Come to my room. I want to fool around a bit." He smiles and winks at me before going up the stairs. Gross. I turn to Holly who smiles and nods for me to go ahead.

"Eric?" I walk into his room, and then hear the door shut behind me. I turn around and to my surprise, it's not Eric.

"Hello Sydney." Clyde purrs in my ear, sliding his hand down my arm.

"What are you d-doing?" I stuttered. I was struggling to hold back the scream that I was dying to let out. Eric had lured me into a trap.

"Oh nothing now lay down on the bed." He commands me. My hands cover my mouth to keep back my sobs as I walk over to the bed and lay down flat on my back. Eric was going to let Clyde rape me, just like that.

"I've always wanted to know how you felt under me, and now's my chance." He grinned wickedly. I squeezed my eyes shut as his hands went up my dress and he skimming over my thigh.

"Mm, you feel nice." He chuckled.

"Please don't do this," I begged him.

"You should know that begging will get you nowhere." He told me. It was true, begging wasn't going to do anything for me. But maybe I could find some way out.

"Eric won't like this." I said to him.

"Eric set this up," he replied and squeezed my thigh.

"Did he really?" I cock an eyebrow, wondering if his words were true.

"Yes," he says as he sits me up and zips down my dress.

"Eric!" I screamed.

"Crap. I owe you fifty dollars Eric." He backs away from me and Eric emerges from the bathroom.

"You made a bet?" I yelled, furious at them both.

"Yup, I was trying to see if you would call out to me for help." He smirked.

"So you would have let him rape me if I didn't?" I asked.

"Yeah," He shrugged and walked over to Clyde who hands him fifty dollars. Wow, so I'm just so rag doll they pass back and forth? Clyde leaves the room and Eric walks over to me.

"Helen let me check your test," Eric blurted.

"Yeah, I'm not pregnant." I replied.

"Actually, you are."

"It said *negative*!" I objected.

"It said *positive*," he stated.

"But I let Holly pee on my stick!" As soon as the words left my mouth, I slapped my hand over my mouth and regretted opening it.

"So the truth comes out." He smirked.

"Eric, please," I begged, hoping he'd let me keep it.

"I had already agreed to let you keep it," he says simply.

"Really?" I gasp.

"It's mine after all. Clyde is careless and doesn't care for children. But I do." He smiles. And at that moment, I knew Eric had a heart.

"On one condition…"

I sucked in a deep breath, prepared for his offer.

"You marry me…"

Crap.

Chapter 5

My body felt heavier all of a sudden, like I couldn't hold it.

"You're joking right?" I said, hopeful that this was just all one big joke.

"Nope." That's when I passed out.

"Christ! Sydney, wake up!" My face was slapped lightly as my eyes fluttered open.

"What happened?"

"You passed out because of my offer," he said. Oh right, his stupid offer.

"Why? Why do you want to marry me? Why must you keep taking things away from me?" I yelled. My head kept pounding and pounding.

"Because, as long as we're married, I can make sure you stay with me forever," he smiled naturally. He was insane. Mental.

"What is so special about me?" I growl.

" . . . You're breakable." he grins. It takes all within me not to punch him in the face right about now, but I make my face expressionless so he won't be satisfied with my reaction.

"We'll see about that," I scoff and get up from the bed.
"What's your answer?"
"Give me some time to think about it, Eric." I snap.

"I'll give you one day. And if I don't get an answer, I'm aborting that child myself," he tells me. I leave his room and break out in a run. This can't be happening. He can't take away my child, but I can't marry him either.

~~~~

Clyde deprived us of food today, again. And Eric didn't bother giving me any. He said something about me not making up my mind. I didn't want to. I didn't want to give him that title. The title of my husband. He doesn't deserve it. My heart ached knowing that I might have to give up my child. My first child . . . and if I don't get out of here, it might be my last.

"Sydney." I heard a voice and looked to my left to see Helen walking toward me.

"Hey, Helen." I smile.

"Eric told me to come talk to you about the gathering in the auditorium today," she said.

"What gathering? What for?" I asked

"Supposedly, they're bringing more girls." She frowns. They're sickening. I feel so bad for whoever these girls will be.

"This is horrible," I mutter.

"Could be worse, right?" She smiles, hoping to cheer me up, but she doesn't. Nothing could make this better. Poor girls are constantly being kidnapped by these two criminals and their servant, Luke.

"I've got to go." I told her suddenly then took off to the nearest restroom. I hurled up my breakfast, hovering over the toilet seat.

I sobbed sliding slowly down the stall door; it was like my world was crashing down. It hurt so bad. It felt like I was being burned alive.

I held my hand up against my stomach and rubbed it in small circle's. My child wasn't going to be a prisoner. And I'm going to make sure she never knows who her father is. Someone like him shouldn't even get the title.

I wiped away my tears and shuffled out of the stall and up to the sinks. My eyes were red and puffy. I looked horrible. There were still faded bruises on my face from previous encounters with Eric. He's been getting angrier lately, but he only does it to scare me.

I walked out of the restroom and back into the hallway where Helen was waiting outside the door.

"Come on, let's go set up." She smiled and led me downstairs and into the auditorium.
I drifted off amongst the busy girls setting up inside the auditorium. There wasn't much to do, but I still had to help.

What was I going to do? This was tearing me apart. Eric loved making me miserable. This was his opportunity to break me. He had talked about it before, but I didn't really want it to be so soon.

I plopped down in a chair, placing the box of wires in the chair next to me.

"Hey, Sydney, you okay?" Helen walked up to me.

"Fine," I muttered.

"Eric told me…about the baby." she revealed. I turned to her.

"Did he also tell you that he's making me choose between my child and him? Either I marry him to keep her or him, or I don't and he takes it away from me," I explain.

"Oh my…Sydney, you can't marry Eric. Your time here would be much harder. He wouldn't let up," she told me.
"So you're telling me to get rid of it?" I snapped.

"Sydney. You want a good life for your children, right?"

"Of course."

"Eric won't only abuse you, but he'll abuse the child. If he wants you to do something, he'll use the child against you." She had a good point, but it only made me upset.

"Not if I go free."

"How Sydney? Only one girl can make it out, we don't even know what's out there, or where we even are."

"Thanks Helen." I snap and stand up, walking away from her. She doesn't get it. She's been here too long. Brainwashed, like the others. There's always a way out.

"Everyone, we would like you to meet the new girls that will be joining our big happy family." Eric spoke through the mic.

I was seated in the fifth row, so I had a pretty nice view of the girls, who right now, had bags over their faces. Eric and Clyde love to surprise people, don't they?

"Helen, would you do the honor of removing their masks?" Eric asked Helen kindly. He was such a good actor.

"Of course, Eric." Helen forced a smile and walked over to the first girl. There were four total. Helen lifted the bag off of her face, and the girl's hair flowed down like a waterfall. She had more than enough hair. The girl was free of her bindings and the first thing she did was move her hair away from her face.

She had big green eyes, like those of a mouse and what looked like natural-blonde hair. Her lips were quivering, and she looked a little younger than I, maybe fourteen. But her skin was as pale, like she had been lying in the snow.

The second girl's bag was removed. Her hair was a raven colored bob. She was flawless; milky white skin, crystal blue eyes and a slender frame.

The third girl had her bag removed. She was also very beautiful, and it seems like Eric and Clyde were hanging around a fashion industry when they kidnapped this bunch.

The girl wore straight, shoulder-length brown hair. Her eyes were (from what I could tell) a light brown or a hazel. She had strong cheekbones and full lips.

The last girl was revealed. She looked rough; her eyes were bruised, probably due to a punch to the face. Her red hair was matted across her face with sweat dripping down her forehead. She was covered in dirt from head-to-toe. She must have put up a fight.

"Laura, Iris, Jada, and Frankie," Clyde spoke, pointing to each girl in order and giving them their new names.

"Round of applause for your new sisters!" Eric smiled and began clapping.

"Now everyone get back to work!" Clyde ordered, and everyone stood and began filing out of the auditorium.

"Sydney, take Laura and Frankie on a tour of the building, and then meet me back here." Eric smiled, though I knew he was only keeping up the nice act to keep everyone clueless of his devilish ways.

"Wait, you guys aren't going to-"

"Clyde has Iris and Jada. And I'm choosing no one." he cuts me off, giving me a "don't be so obvious" look.

"Got it," I said before leading Laura and Frankie out of the auditorium.

I took them first to the cafeteria, then the cinema, then into the elevator. Once the door shuts, I feel a light tap on my shoulder.
I see Laura with a fearful look spread across her face.

"What is this place? And why are there so many girls? I need to get home!" she rushed out, tears streaming down her cheeks.

"I'll explain later . . . um, just . . . stop crying for now, okay?" I told her, not sure how to comfort her. No one comforted me, and I hadn't even cried when I arrived here.

We arrived on their floor, which was the sixth. A few girls had stopped and stared at us. A few sent me hateful glares.

"Your room is this way," I said as we turned right and went down the hallway. Eric had said that they would share a room. It was the last empty one. Other than that, we had run out of rooms, which meant they wouldn't take any more girls. That brought me a little joy.

"Here it is. You two will be sharing," I said to them as I unlocked their door.

"Sydney, right?" Frankie turned to me.

"Yes,"

"Can I talk to you for a moment?" I nodded and we let Laura go inside while we talked in the hall.

"How was it possible for them to kidnap so many girls without getting caught?" she questioned; her curiosity was evident.

"I'm not really sure," I told her honestly.

"Is there any way out?" I shook my head and she frowned.

"Well, only if your name is drawn, other than that, I've got no idea." I said.
"It's two guys against a bunch of girls, we can easily escape!"

"No, our bands, they contain some sort of kill switch, the system is impossible to surpass." I explained.

"There's a way, there's always a way." She muttered and went inside her room, closing the door behind her.

"Sydney! Sydney! Wake up, now!" I was awakened by the sound of Jane's voice. I rose and turned to her. She looked scared and worried.

"You have to stop them!" she yelled and pulled on my arm.

"What's going on? Stop who?" I asked as she pulled me out of the door.

"Eric and Clyde; they say there's too many girls, so they're just going to slaughter fifty of them!" My mouth hung low.

"You're the only one that can convince Eric! Please!" She said while dragging me to the elevator.

We arrived on the first floor and got out. And lined up against the wall were the fifty innocent girls. Clyde stood with some kind of rifle in his hands, prepared to shoot, while Eric stood close by.

"Stop!" I yelled. Eric and Clyde turned towards me. I stomped up to Eric and got right in his face.

"You can't do this, this is wrong. I'm begging you to not do this." I pleaded.

"Begging, huh? How about we make a little arrangement, yeah? You, marry me. And they live." He smirked down at me. My stomach dropped and I felt like screaming. This was his doing. He was only doing this so I could marry him.

"Eric I-"

"You have ten seconds before I let Clyde here let off some steam on these targets." I was on the verge of tears and could feel reality crashing down on me.

"Five more seconds." he reminded me. I sighed and gave up.

"Fine, I'll marry you." I spoke.

"Good; fire." Before I could stop the horrible spring of events, bodies began dropping to the ground; there was a high-pitched ringing in my ears and their screams echoing through the building. Blood tainted the floors and stained the perfectly painted white walls. Within a quick second I had fallen to my knees, horror whipped across my face like a belt.

This was it, this was me breaking.

Chapter 6

"No!" I jolted up, sweat pecking my forehead like a morning kiss. I looked over at Jane who had only stirred a bit at my outburst. This had been my third nightmare this week.

All I could see were those horrified faces belonging to the bodies that were now lifeless. Fifty girls; fifty innocent girls that Eric had used as bait for me. It was my fault, all my fault. I can't think straight anymore. All I can think about is how I've caused all this trouble for everyone. I should just abort it. She or he shouldn't have to live in this kind of place.

"Good; fire."

Those words had been echoing through my mind for countless days, haunting me in my daydreams.

I looked out the barred window. I hadn't even noticed that the sun was coming up. Was I sitting here long?

I stood up and walked out of the room. An arm was slung around my shoulder. It was Eric, I could tell by the familiar scent of liquor and fruity candles. He was drunk. He'd been upset that I hadn't slept in his room last night, so he slapped me and ordered me to leave.

"How's my little baby-maker doing?" He slurred.
"Just fine," I muttered sarcastically.
"Good, good. I want you to know that you're sleeping in my room tonight, and if you have one of those damn nightmares again, I'll abort your baby." He threatened. He'd already had a taste of my constant nightmares.

"Today, you'll be working…working on-with Helen." He pushed me and then walked away. I picked myself up off my knees and went downstairs. Lately, Eric has been letting me work with Helen, which is better than spending my whole day with him.

I shuffled down the stairs, girls pushing past me. Everyone still hated me. But I had gotten used to it. Everything had a numbness to it. It was like nothing bothered me anymore. When Eric forced himself on me, I just lay back and let my thoughts roll away, except when he made me interact with him, which was usually half-assed. And his constant beating weren't as bad as they were before.

"S-Sydney." I turned around and saw Iris heading toward me. I moved to the side, getting out of everyone's way.

"Hey Iris." I forced a smile. The first time I saw her she was afraid, yet still held life in her eyes, and now her eyes looked restless along with her body seeing that she was now Clyde's favorite toy.

"I wanted to know if you'd like to sit with me at lunch. Frankie and Laura are joining us too." She said politely.

"What about Jada?" I asked, practically knowing the answer.

"Clyde is keeping her for himself." She muttered her voice cracking.

"Oh…sure I'll join you all." I smiled.

"Great." She gave me a small smile, her eyes bringing forth more tears.

"Excuse me." She said and ran off to the bathrooms. I continued downstairs to Helen's office. When I walked in she was on a telephone with someone. Wait…is she calling for help? "H-hold on one second-okay thank you. Hi, Sydney, if you could just give me a moment, I'll be right with you." she told me.

I walked into the next room, standing close to the door frame to listen in on their conversation.

"Okay, I'm back…No, no one's listening…I've received more information…yes. Clyde was going on about some forest near Oklahoma last night when he was drunk." she spoke quietly. What about the cameras? Won't they see her on the phone?

I peeked around the wall and saw the security camera, being covered up by what looked like a photo.

"I can't tell you much more, but I'm sure we're somewhere in Oklahoma or near it at least. Okay, I'll speak with you later John-I love you too-alright, goodbye." She hung up the phone and unplugged it from the wall and carried it into the storage closet.

"Helen," I said as she walked out of the storage closet.

"Sydney were you listening?" she asked, horror spread across her face.

"Yes, who were you talking to?" I asked her. She grabbed my arm and pulled me into the storage closet.

"You need to forget everything you heard me saying on the phone. If Eric or Clyde or even Luke have the slightest idea that something's going on, they'll ask you, because you're the only one I'm around all day! They'll question you. And maybe threaten to kill your child if you don't give them what they want. Forget everything!" She pleaded in a hushed tone.

"Helen I won't-"

"Everything!" She hissed. I nodded and she let out a deep breath. Helen seemed weak and vulnerable, but she was hiding a damn phone in the storage closet.

"Now sort out these files. I have some more abortions to take care of," she told me and left me to my organizing. I grabbed the box of files and began sorting them. I'd done this before. I just have to collect loose papers and place them in ABC order.

I started with the box labeled, "Records I-M." I gathered up all the loose sheets of paper, and then picked up the first folder.

~~~~

I reached for the last file, my eyes becoming heavier by the second. I grabbed it, but it was surprisingly lighter than the others. I looked at the name on the front and saw Helen Martin. Was this actually Helen's file? I opened it, looking through the papers.

Helen Martin

Tiffany Moree

Born: 16, November 1990.

Parents/Guardians: Arnold R. Martin, Karin Lane

Siblings: Arnold R. Martin Jr., Joseph Martin, K

The rest of the document was ripped to pieces. Who was K? Another sibling? Why would someone rip her sibling's names off? There has to be more. I checked the next page, but it was blank. Oh well. I pushed the folders to the side to make room for the folder, but noticed another folder trapped underneath all of the other folders.

I lifted a few folders up to slide my fingers under and grab the folder. I read the name on the front.

"Kimberly Martin."

Helen's sister was kidnapped with her? I couldn't stop the sudden urge to open the folder and search through its contents.

I got up and peeked out the door. Helen wasn't around. I sat back down on the floor grabbing the folder and opened it.

The first thing I saw was a journal. It was leather and looked a little old and tattered. I opened it and read the first page.
Day 1: The Big Project

My family has betrayed Joseph and me. They're sending us to a mental hospital. They are all idiots. A few weeks ago, I stumbled upon an old mansion. It looks fixable. It's well hidden too.

Joseph thinks we should hide out there. I think so too. That way we won't be taken away.

I stole my college fund from my parents. We could hire some people to fix up the mansion, then pay them off to keep quiet. This could work.

I don't know what to do with the mansion. Maybe I could house runaways like Joseph and myself.

It'd be for a good cause…yes.

Mansion? Wait is this the journal of the original mansion owner? It couldn't have been Eric. His brother is Luke, and there's no explanation for why Clyde's here. Maybe this could show me a way out, and maybe I could finally be-

"Sydney." Helen said. My back faced her so I had enough time to hide the journal.

"Yes?" I said casually as I stood up.

"What are you doing with that folder?" she asked, referring to Kimberly's folder.
"I was putting it away-"

89

"Give it to me," she ordered me, a panicked look in her eyes. I grabbed the folder and handed it to her. She glared at me before walking out of the storage closet.

"Helen what are you hiding?" I asked her as I followed right behind her.

"That's enough organizing for today Sydney, I won't need you tomorrow. Have a good night." She faked a smile and left. I quickly went back for the journal, then put the box back and headed for my room.

Day 8: A New Plan

Everything is going as planned. The building is almost complete. My parents are out of the picture. Joseph and I decided to bring our little sisters with us, Kimberly and Helen. They can't go into the foster system and we can't have them running to the cops either.

I met a friend the other day. He says he's good with girls, taking care of them that is. He has little sisters of his own. He said he'll bring them along. This could work out great. I mean, we have plenty of space.

I hadn't noticed that the name Joseph was the name of Helen's brother. So this is Arnold's journal. Wait so they were the ones who discovered the mansion, which means Helen wasn't kidnapped. And her sister wasn't either. They were brought here to live. But where are her brothers?

"Hey Sydney," Jane's voice caused me to quickly slide the journal under my pillow.

"Hey Jane," I sighed.

"What were you reading?" she questioned.

"Nothing…just a list of things I need to complete tomorrow." I lied.

"In a journal? Whatever. When you're ready to tell me the truth, then tell me. It's your secret, not mine." She sighs and gets under her blankets.

I didn't want to keep this a secret from Jane, but if she got involved, she might end up like all of the others. I'm not letting anyone else get killed because of me. I have too many problems as it is. This journal will probably show me my way out. Helen's hiding something major, and she doesn't want anyone to find out. And the whole phone thing has still got me quite on edge. She's trying to find a way out, yet she's hiding so many secrets.

"Sydney." Someone knocks on the door.

It's Jada.

"Yes?" I said sitting up in my bed.

"Eric is requesting your services," she informed me. Of course he is. He's starting to piss me off, but I can't show it, I can't let him think that he's affecting me, yet he has done so much already.

I nod and follow her out. As we're walking, she suddenly stops.

"After you leave Eric's room, go into the elevator. We'll be waiting there. Now act casual and continue walking," she whispered to me, and then continued walking. What's this about? Who's we? She takes me to Eric's room, and then dismisses herself. I walk inside Eric's room, knowing it is unlocked.

"Sit down on the bed." He orders me as he begins to pace back and forth. I obeyed and sat waiting for him to tell me to take off my clothes, like he does every night.

"I've been very hard on you lately," he said. I was shocked; when did Eric become sympathetic?

"I'm usually nice, but ever since I've been with you, all of my anger and hatred have been directed towards you. I'm not even angry at you most of the time. I want to apologize." Another shocking sentence.

"Uh…I forgive you…" I lied. It was what he wanted to here so I might as well say it since he's acting so weird.

"Good. I'm going to be nicer, not just to you but to everyone. I want to go back to the old me." He told me, almost seeming sincere.

"Do you like Luke?" He blurted.

"No, why?" I say truthfully. I don't know what kind of "like" he meant, but I didn't like Luke any more than I liked Eric, which meant I disliked the both of them.

"Okay. Um…remove your clothes." He orders me, although he sounds unsure. Nicer Eric my ass.

After Eric had done what he wanted with me, he sent me on my way. And like Jada told me, I met her inside the elevator, along with four other familiar faces: Iris, Laura, Frankie, and Jane.

"Okay Sydney, we heard about your attempt to escape and how you had almost made it out," Frankie said to me. No, I wasn't doing this. I'm not going to escape unless it's by myself, no one else could be involved.
"Guys-"

"Hear us out Sydney" Laura begged. I sighed and crossed my arms letting them continue.

"You may have thought your plan was well thought out, but it had a lot of mistakes. You took the key from a guy who's always sober. You gave him time to figure it out. You guys didn't know that anyone besides Clyde and Eric worked here. And you involved other people." Frankie listed, slightly hurting me with each word.

"I think I know all of my mistakes, Frankie, I've beaten myself up about them multiple times." I retorted.
"Well anyways, I think if we all work together, we can get at least one person out of here. And to make sure neither of us get killed. We all pretend to hate each other." A small smile formed on my face.

"This is going to take a lot of brainwork," Laura says.

"But then again, I do have this." I pulled the journal out of my pocket and hold it up.

"What is that?" Iris asked.

"It's the journal that belonged to the original owner of the mansion. There could be a map, or a clue to a way out of here," I told them.

"So digging a hole with a spoon underground is out of the question?" Jane joked.

"This plan has to be perfect. Something no one will expect. But we have to continue living our everyday lives in this shit-hole. No one can suspect a thing, especially not Eric or Clyde. Luke, we can't trust him, but he seems to dislike Eric, so we can probably turn him against Eric. We also can't involve Helen." Everyone paused.

"Wait, why not Helen?" Jada asked.

"She's hiding things, big things. We can't involve her. She's like Eric and Clyde's puppet, she'll do anything to survive."

"Okay, we meet every week in this elevator, same time. If we meet too often, someone will know something's up." Jane determined. We all agreed then went to our separate rooms. If this all works out, I'll know there's hope for these girls. Hope for their families. And hope for my child.

Chapter 7

One month. That was how far along I was. Helen says that I'm doing fine and I'm very healthy. She mentioned that I should eat plenty of fruits and vegetables and stay on some special vitamins she gave me. It had also been a little over a month since I had been trapped in this prison. Even if I was trapped here like everyone else, most of the girls were still upset because of my many privileges.

Iris had told me about some rumor of a group girl's plotting to gang up on me so I could miscarry. I mentioned it to Eric who warned everyone that if they hurt me physically, he would personally put a bullet in their heads. That put me at ease for my child, but Eric was still a douche and I was still his little sex toy. I hated how he could just force himself on me, knowing that I'm with child.

The girls and I haven't had any more ideas about escaping. We don't really know how we'll get one person out of here without getting caught. And if we're somewhere in Oklahoma, which by the way, is two states away from my home in Mississippi, then it'd be a long trip back.

Breakfast was about to start soon, so I headed downstairs, blending in with the crowd of girls. I was about to go to the table that I usually sat at with Iris and the rest, but knew that they we were all supposed to be sitting separately. I sat towards the middle next to a couple of girls who were much younger than I. They were talking about boys back home and silly stuff like that.

Eric and Clyde walked in, but someone followed behind them, and it was Luke. I guess they're finally introducing him officially, he was usually cooped up in that control room 24/7.

"Good morning, whores." Clyde greeted with a grin on his face.

"Good morning Clyde," the whole room greeted back. I rolled my eyes, Clyde always knew how to greet people properly.

"Good morning, girls." Eric smiled politely. He's so fake.

"Good morning, Eric." Everyone replied back, many with their usual flirtatious tones.

"Everyone, this is Luke. He's responsible for creating this entire system, including the bands you all wear on your wrists. Say good morning girls." Eric announced.

"Good morning, Luke." The cafeteria chorused.

"Um…good morning," Luke greeted in a nervous manner, and then sat down. He seemed a little awkward, but what did I care?

We proceeded through the morning ritual, waiting for Clyde and Eric, and now Luke to finish their meals. And after they were done they stood up. Clyde announced that we could all eat breakfast, which was good (for everyone else). But Luke wasn't leaving the cafeteria just yet. He headed through the tables and down my aisle. This was not good.

"Sydney," Luke said. I frowned and turned to him. I could already hear the rumors and jealous taunts.

"Yes?" I grumbled.

"Meet me in the control room after you finish. Eric wants you to help me out with some things." he whispered, although the few girls that were nearby could hear every word.

"Okay. Now, go away." I urged. He left the cafeteria and the food was handed out except for mine. The girls who were giving out the plates had purposely skipped over me.

"Tell Eric and we'll kill you," One whispered in my ear.
"Do it then, I dare you," I stood up so fast that the girl jumped back and I narrowed my eyes at her.

"You are nothing, Sydney. No one likes you. Why don't you just die in a hole somewhere and leave Eric alone?" another hissed.

"You guys think Eric is so nice and good, don't you? Well you don't have to deal with him twenty-four seven! You haven't been hit by him, or punched or slapped by him! You haven't been raped by him! And you don't have to marry the person that you hate! None of you guys know what I go through. Yet you hate me because I was chosen by Eric. Take Eric, because I don't want him!" I screamed. Everyone's eyes were on me. Some of them looked as if they believed me, and others didn't. I felt the horrid sensation of the band sending electric shocks through my veins. I fell onto my knees and stayed there until the pain ceased. Once it stopped, I got up and ran to the control room.

"You weren't supposed to tell them that. Eric's going to kill you." Luke told me as I walked up to him.

"Like I care," I scoffed and rolled my eyes.

"You should try to remember that you're carrying a child Sydney, and Eric can do whatever he wants to you and to it." He reminded me.
"I don't need you to worry about me Luke, for all I know, you could be just like him." I responded angrily before sitting down in a nearby chair.

"And what if I want to worry-"

"Don't do that. Don't act like you care about me, when I know you don't. You're like his little minion; Helen too. It's pathetic. I don't need someone like you to worry about a girl like me. I've made it this far, and I plan on making it out of here." It felt good to snap at someone without getting yelled at or hit. I liked voicing my own opinion.

"I know that. But what else can I do? Leave? And go where? My parents are dead and I have no friends outside of this place. I have no choice." He sighed and sat down in a chair next to me.

"You can start fresh. I mean, what if this place goes down and the cops find out about it. You, Eric, and Clyde will all be arrested. Then what? Spend your whole life in jail because you couldn't grow enough balls to stand up and be a man and leave this place? Luke, you have lots of potential," I said, slowly trying to convince him. This was my chance to get Luke on my side and I wasn't going to pass it up.

"I don't know how. I've been with Eric for so long, I don't know how to make it on my own," He admitted. Inside I wanted to pity him, assume that he was innocent in all this but I didn't have time for pity, I needed him to get us out of here.

"That's exactly what he wants; for you to depend on him so much that you won't want to leave. But you can't fall for his…his mind games," I stood to my feet walking closer to him as I continued to talk. "Do you really want Eric to control every aspect of your life forever? You have to break away some day,"

"What do you suggest, Sydney the guru?" He said jokingly.

"If you help us escape-"

"You know I can't do that…Eric would find out and then I'd be the one trying to stay alive," He deadpanned. I groaned inwardly. Luke was too weak, but there had to be some way to convince him to do this. The idea came almost too quickly, and in seconds I was inches away from his face.

"If you just stick with me, I'll figure something out, a plan that won't endanger any of us." I whispered. His eyes were drawn to my lips that were mere inches away from his. Bingo.

"I thought you hated me…" he trailed off slowly being pulled into my little trap.

"What gave you that idea?" I said, before leaning forward, pecking his lips lightly. His hands cupped my face and my arms were wrapping around his neck as I pulled him closer. It was like tossing a lion a steak, his lips were hungry and his actions matched as his hand slid down my thigh gripping it like his life depended on it. I felt my pulse speeding up in the heat of the moment, but for some reason it didn't feel right. I wanted to stop his hands and push him away from me, but I continued kissing him for the sake of meeting my goal.

He came to an immediate halt, backing away from me. "Helen," Luke mumbled and I turned around seeing Helen standing in the doorway. She had a curt smile on her face and wiggled her finger for me to come with her.

"We'll talk later." I whispered to him before walking out the door past Helen. She followed closely behind me and when we walked down an empty corridor she yanked me back with a stern look plastered on her face.

"Don't play with his heart, Sydney. Luke is still a kid and he loves hard but hates harder; when he gets tired of Eric taking advantage of you, he might do something about it and so will Eric. If it means breaking you, Eric will hurt or kill anyone that means something to you, even his own brother." My eyes widen and I stopped in my tracks.
"It's nothing serious Helen," I assured her, knowing I was both lying to her and myself. She

walks me to Eric's room and I thanked her before going inside.

"Hello my little Sydney. How are we today?" He smiles, like he has no care in the world.

"Perfect," I spat.

"Watch the tone, watch the tone," he warned. "You know the routine. Remove your clothes," He smirked. I had frozen in place, feeling myself getting upset suddenly. I didn't want to, my body was tired and so was I and before I knew it, I had started crying.

"I've had enough Eric. I can't do this anymore. Take someone else, anyone else and I'll do anything you want, I'll marry you without any complaints, I'll stay here forever…just please don't make me do this anymore." That's what he wanted to hear. He wanted to hear me give up and beg and plead. He wanted to know how broken I was. So that's what I'd give him, but it was partially a part of my plan.

"Sounds tempting, but it's not like I'm just going to stop having sex with you. You're too beautiful. And you give me pleasure," He grinned.
"I wasn't going to let you complain, either. And you do everything I want already. So basically, you're just bargaining with nothing," He added.

"It's rape," I muttered.

"What was that?" He said, his hands clenching into tight fists.

"It's…freaking rape! Not sex!" I yelled louder. In the next second I had been slapped to the ground with a burning sensation from my cheek.

"It's not rape! I am not a rapist! You know you want me, Sydney!" he hollered.

"You are a rapist, Eric! You even threatened to rape me! I never asked you for this!" I screamed at him.

"Leave." He demanded through a clenched jaw. I stood up and walked out of his room. He slammed the door behind me which was followed by crashing and banging coming from inside his room.

I hated him so much, I wanted him dead.

I walked back to my room, which was absent of Jane luckily. I needed to read more of that journal I found. I sat down on my bed, taking the journal out from underneath my pillow and opened it to the last page I had read.

Day 24
My contractor and I had countless conversations on ways that I could build more. I can build more floors. I can store tons of runaways. My parents

*would be so proud of me, if they weren't so
incompetent and judgmental they'd be alive to see
how much true potential I have.*

*Joseph is still young; I'll be able to get him to
learn about computers and coding so he can
create the perfect system. Technology wasn't my
specialty, but if I got him to do it, it'd be a lot
easier on me and Clyde.*

Day 40

*Nothing makes sense anymore. Clyde's been
bringing in so many girls, but they're not
runaways. I guess its fine, but what am I supposed
to do with them? And why are they so afraid? This
isn't how it's supposed to go! Why can't anything
go how I want it? Everything has to be perfect, I
need to have more money, this place won't last if I
don't get money somehow.*

Day 68

*A new name, A new me. Eric was now my name. I
think everyone should have new names once they
get here. Joseph could be Luke, and Clyde, well
Clyde likes his name so I guess he can keep it.
Terry tells me that it's better if I change my name;
he's a good friend of Clyde's and has been
sponsoring my building for a while. He gives good
advice, but he can be a little controlling. I'm the
boss, not him!*

My eyes were popping out of my head. This was Eric's journal. Eric killed his parents, and took his brother and two sisters. Helen…is Eric's sister. They've hid it from everyone this whole time. Was Helen's sob story just an act? But she seemed like she was trying to get out of here.

I can't trust anyone from now on, only my true friends.

I feel like I have the upper hand now, like I'm one step ahead of Eric and Clyde. Now that I have this journal I can find a way to escape this place.

I skimmed through the pages of the journal, hoping to find a map or something. I searched the journal front and back, but there's nothing. I sigh and slide the journal under my pillow. I lie down flat on my back and stare up at the ceiling. I won't be a prisoner, especially not Eric's prisoner.

I'll make it home. Back to my old life, my friends, my family. We'll be happy again. Because I know they're going through hell right now searching for me. But then again home wasn't happy at all when I was taken. My parents were struggling in their marriage, my friends had betrayed me; going back to all that, especially with a child would just be adding to the hell I left behind, but this wasn't just about me, it was about everyone in this place.

Chapter 8

Scott's POV

Flashback

I was sitting beside Mark and a few of his friends as they talked about some lame party that happened last week. Well it wasn't lame to them because they always got hammered and ended up drunk calling me in the middle of the night.

I looked around the school yard, everyone was so excited to leave, mainly because of another pointless party that was being thrown.

"Scott." My attention turned to Lisa who stood there with Sydney.

"What's up?" I asked. Lisa batted her eyelashes and flipped her coffee colored waves. Who knows why she acted so flirtatious around guys, probably daddy issues. I didn't understand why Sydney always hung out with her when she was always calling her a bitch behind her back.

"Sydney is coming over to my house." she informed me. This was obviously a sad cover up attempt so they could go to the party tonight. Freshman year Sydney never liked that sort of shit, we were closer back then, but Lisa squeezed her away into the picture and corrupted her with her social mind-set.

"Okay," I drawled. She smiled and touched my shoulder. "Make sure you tell your parents that too, okay?" I shrugged her off and shot her a quick nod, getting her to leave. I didn't care what they did, just as long as I didn't get in trouble for it, other than that, Sydney could do whatever the hell she wanted. But I couldn't shake the feeling that something was wrong. That Sydney should just walk home with me, but it was silly to think something bad was going to happen, I shook the feeling away and turned over to Mark who was immaturely imitating a dolphin.

I looked down at my phone which had 1:45 displayed across the top. I slapped Mark's shoulder, and he turned around. I showed him my phone and everyone soon stood up and began walking.

My friends always seemed to bring up some immature topic about video games and playboy magazines on our walks home and somehow I drowned them out.

I waved goodbye to Mark before he continued down the block. I opened my front door and went inside.

"Scott, Sydney is that you?" My mom called out.

"Just me, Mom," I replied and slipped off my shoes. Mom walked out from the kitchen holding a mixing bowl. Her hair was slightly dusty from the flour that seemed to be everywhere else except for the bowl. I chuckled at the sight. She was never a baker nor much of cook either.

"Where's Sydney?" she questioned, wiping sweat from her forehead.
"With Lisa," I answered and headed for the stairs, but my mom quickly stopped me.

"What are they doing?" she raised an eyebrow, expecting me to spill like I occasionally did. But this time, I would lie, just this once.

"Studying for some big math exam; Sydney said it was really important and something about a scholarship." I lied, smoothly.

"Oh, well okay. Dinner will be ready in a few, do your homework." Mom said and kissed my cheek, then went off into the kitchen. She should know me well enough to know that last minute homework was my personal specialty.

I checked my cell phone seeing that it was 7:30. Mom had been in the kitchen for over five hours making some meal from hell. She couldn't cook to save her life, but I loved her anyways. I heard a light knock on my door. I got up and opened it. I looked down seeing Maddie pulling off one of her innocent smiles that probably meant that she wanted something from me.

"Can I borrow a dollar?" She asked politely. Who knew what she needed with all the money she asked for but my answer was usually the same every time.

"No, now scram." I smirked and ruffled up her hair, which she hated. She groaned and stomped into her room.

"Dinner's ready!" My mom called from downstairs. I looked over to my brother's door, which was closed. He and his wife Vanessa were visiting for the week. My parents were just so excited that they'd be having their first grandchild.

I walked up to the door and was prepared to knock but quickly walked away after hearing the disturbing grunts and moans coming from their bedroom. I am scarred for life.

My dad and Maddie were already at the table with their plates in front of them. I sat down at my usual spot, which was next to Sydney who wasn't here yet and probably wouldn't be for the rest of the night. Knowing her, she'd probably find some way to convince mom to let her spend the weekend with Lisa.
"Call your sister and check if she's heading home," Mom told me. I grabbed my phone from

my pocket and clicked on her contact name. It rang a few times, and then went to voice mail.

"She didn't pick up. I'm sure she's fine mom." I assured her. Mom looks hesitant but doesn't say anything else. My brother and his wife soon join us.

"Have fun up there?" I whispered to Blake, whose face went red. He punched my shoulder and glared down at his food. I chuckled and continued eating my rice. His hits were more bearable now that I was older.

Dinner went on with loud and joyful conversations about the new baby and stuff like that. I only made comments occasionally. The whole family dinner thing every night gets tiring after a while and I gave up on trying to make conversation, seeing that everyone else had better things to talk about.

"Clear off the table, Scott. I'm going to call Lisa's mother and see if Sydney has left yet." I groaned but began clearing off the table, but tried to listen in on the conversation between Lisa's mother and my mom.

"Hello. Hi Evelyn! Yes I'm doing fine, the kids are fine…yes I know Scott told me…did she just leave or is she still there? Twenty minutes ago? She should have been here by then…no of course it's not your fault, I'm sure Sydney is fine…okay, talk to you later…okay bye." Mom hung up the phone forcefully.

"Call Sydney now! If she's somewhere else so help me I will ground her for all of eternity" My mom growled and stormed off. I jogged upstairs and went to Sydney's room. Most times she would climb through the window and into her room so she could keep from getting in trouble.

Surprisingly, her room was empty. I quickly dialed her number and let it ring. It rang for a while, and when I heard buzzing coming from her bed, I knew she had left her phone.

"Where the hell are you?" I muttered to myself.

I went back down the stairs and saw my mom standing outside in the door frame.

"Mom…what's wrong?" I asked. She walked forward and out onto the lawn, going out into the street. I saw her pick up something and she walked back.

"This is your sister's backpack, right?" My mom asked, tears welling in her eyes. I nodded. Mom nodded her head. Why was her backpack in the street?

"Call 911 now." She stammered. I tried dialing the numbers, but my hands wouldn't stop shaking. I couldn't escape the feeling that something horrible had probably happened to her and that she never made it home.

Mom told dad and they told Blake, Maddie, and Vanessa. This was all my fault. If I had just went with my instincts and told Sydney to come home with me, none of this would be happening.

I really hoped she was alright. I couldn't live with myself knowing something bad happened to her. She had to be with Lisa or one of her other friends. But that doesn't explain her backpack in the middle of the road. She wouldn't have just left it there, she loves that backpack.

I suddenly felt the phone slip out of my fingers; dad had taken it from me and called the cops. I couldn't escape the constant feeling that something bad occurred. Nothing felt right.

Chapter 9

"You have got to be kidding me," Jane said looking at the updated score sheet. I rolled my eyes and leaned up against the wall. Everyone was going to slaughter me.

"You have one thousand points, Sydney. You're getting out of here," She muttered more to herself than me.

"That's the thing that I'm most worried about." I admit to her. She looks at me, confused.

"What are you saying?" she asks. Luckily, we were in the stalls where the camera's only showed the sinks and outside the showers.

"I'm just saying, why would they let us go so freely? They would never risk getting caught like that," I say to her.

"So you're saying they don't leave. They just . . . disappear? Come on, Sydney, get real." Jane scoffs.

"No, you get real. Do you really think that Clyde and Eric expect us all to just leave this place and not try to call the cops?" I asked. She paused for a while.

"Okay, now I believe what you're saying, but what's the purpose of the points?" She asks as we both step out of our separate stalls, not looking at each other to show we were talking.

"To give us false hope, I don't know, I read more of the journal last night. Eric had mentioned how Clyde was changing things and some other guy named Terry, maybe they have something to do with how everyone got kidnapped." I said. She doesn't say anything else and dries her hands then leaves, and then I do the same.

Jane may not believe me completely, and I doubt the others will, so I'll keep this little thought to myself for now.

"Sydney, please report to the theater immediately." I hear the intercom and it shuts off with a click. Well I guess I'm going to the theater. I took the elevator, seeing that the stairs were starting to wear me out a lot lately and Helen tells me not to push myself too much. What if my calves start to swell? Then I'd have cancels. Pregnancy is so weird and its symptoms have gotten more intense since I'm two months along.

When I reach the door leading into the theater, I open it and walk inside, closing it back. I feel warm hands wrap around me.

"Eric, what's going…?"

"It's Luke." I instantly fly out of Luke's arms. There's part of me that can't trust him because he's actually Joseph, but I can't let him know I know.

"Sorry, I didn't mean to scare you." He smiled then walked towards me.

"It's fine, I just thought-never mind…what did you call me here for?" I asked.

"You're here to help me with the projector." He stated.

"What am I supposed to do? I'm not even sure how to work a projector, let alone fix one." I told him. He glanced at me and grinned.

"It's alright, I'll show you." He grabbed my hand and pulled me over to where he was fixing the projector. Being near him made me uncomfortable, he was lying about his true identity and he probably helped Eric get rid of their parents. I was seducing a possible murderer, yet I was the one feeling guilty.

"All we're doing is removing the headlamp, so first-"

"Couldn't you handle this by yourself; you seem to know what you're doing?" I said, trying to not make it obvious that I didn't want to be here.

"Well I needed an excuse to see you." I groaned inwardly. How could someone like him be so incredibly sweet? He stood up in front of me putting his arms around me.

"You should have called me in earlier, lunch is in five minutes." I told him, slipping out of his hold.

"Damn, tomorrow then?" I nodded, although I honestly didn't want to be near him or touch him or have anything to do with him. Every time he looked at me all I could see was Eric and it made me want to scream.

He pulled my chin to his lips briefly before letting me go. I gave him a fake smile and walked out of the theater. I dodged a bullet with that.

After exiting the theater I spotted Frankie, who was being approached by a couple of girls, one who I recognized as Courtney. She's probably trying to start trouble again. I was about to walk over to her, but I stopped myself. No one's supposed to know me and Frankie are friends.

I walked past, sending her a sad stare. She winked at me before I saw her punch Courtney in her jaw. Courtney went down like a domino. Many girls had seen it, and a few were running to attack her. Soon enough, a crowd formed and I couldn't see anything. I left the crowd and went upstairs and into my room.

When I entered my room, it was strangely full of people. And by strangely, I mean it was full of people. The first person I recognized was Eric, standing there admiring a white gown. Wait . . . white gown?! Please don't tell me that's-

"Sydney, you made it. Sorry about the mess, I've been working with these girls all morning," He smiled at me. I looked around the room, seeing sewing machines, bits and pieces of fabric and in the center, a beautiful white dress which was most definitely for me.

"Beautiful isn't it? I rounded up a few girls who mentioned they knew how to sew; a couple of hours later, and here we are." He took my hand in his and brought me closer to the wedding gown. It was indescribable.

It was a strapless ball gown with a satin bodice tight around the waist that flowed out below the waistline. It was quite plain but lovely. How did they manage to finish it so quickly?

"How did you guys manage to finish it so quickly?" I asked no one in particular.

"We haven't. There are still many details we have to work on. And the back of the dress is ruined due to a mishap with some string; we still need you to try it on, so we can get the size perfect." One of the girls told me. I nodded at her and

121

looked at Eric who was watching them work with an elated expression. He had never looked so happy before, and I was questioning if this was real or just an act.

 I smiled slightly and turned around to leave the room, but Eric grabbed my arm pulling me back. "Let's walk." He said and held my hand, leading me out the door. I grimaced and walked next to him. Did he have to hold my hand?

"Okay the wedding is going to happen in about a month. I'll have Helen plan everything, so you don't have to stress yourself while you're pregnant." He began, and the whole time he talked I thought about how delusional he was. He's acting as if I actually want this wedding, and that I care about the dress or the details or the wedding at all. He's acting as though I wanted to be married to him.

"Do you have any ideas who you want as your bridesmaids?" He asked me. I shook my head. I couldn't let him know I have any friends, that way there are no connections.

"I thought you and Jane were friends?" He asked.

"Not anymore, she's mad at me for not saving those girls Clyde killed." I lied. He didn't say anything else after that, maybe it's because he felt guilty, who knows.

We ended up circling around the building and then went back into my room, where they had cleared out all the fabrics and needles and my dress. Eric informed me that they had taken it to another room so I could lie down. Eric insisted that I lay down and rested, which I obeyed partially, since I only wanted to look through the journal again.

Day 119
I didn't mean it. I didn't mean it. I didn't mean it! It wasn't me. I didn't know what I was doing. It just happened. I was drunk. Everyone does crazy things when they're drunk, right? But do people rape their own sister when their drunk? I've tainted her! What will Luke say? What will Helen say? I can't let Kimberly tell them, they'll hate me. But I'm the oldest, they can't hate me. I can make them do what I like, like little puppets on strings. Maybe I did mean it. What's happening to me? Why can't I be normal?
Population in facility: 98 girls total.

Day 124
She told them. But she lied and said it was Clyde. Clyde denied it, but Luke and Helen didn't believe him and asked me to kick him out. I told them I wouldn't because Clyde's my best friend, but I told him to stay away from my sister. She cursed at me last night when I came into her room. She started crying because she thought I was going to touch her again. I promised her I wouldn't and that she

should lock her door at night just in case I got drunk and stupid again. I think we're okay now. But nothing can make up for what I did to her. I feel terrible.

Day 130
This isn't happening. No, no, no, no, no, no, no, no! I'm horrible. I killed her. It was me, I killed her! I'm so sorry! Forgive me. Come back! Please! I didn't mean it! I'm sorry! I'm sorry! I'm sorry!

Day 131
The look on her face when I killed her was so shocked. I didn't expect for me to just snap like that. She called me pathetic and weak and a rapist. I'm not a rapist, I was drunk! Kimberly come back, please! I'm sorry. People screamed when I snapped her neck and her body fell limp onto the floor. Helen and Luke found out soon after, but at least now they're afraid, at least now I can control them properly.

Day 167
No one can know what I've done this past year. No one can know who I've killed. I won't write for too much longer. Everyone believes I'm dead, including the police. I just have to lay low for a while.

He raped his own sister? He was seriously messed up in the head, but now I know why he got so angry when I called him a rapist. Maybe I could use that to my benefit.

I closed the journal and slid it under my mattress. I've had to switch my hiding spots frequently now, because Eric's been coming inside my room very often. I can't let him know I have it.

The door opened and looked over to see Jane walking in, her face red and puffy. "Jane what's wrong? What happened?" I asked her filled with concern.

"I'll tell you when we go to bed. We're supposed to not like each other, remember?" I nodded and awkwardly walked out of the room. What is going on around here lately?

When we were told lights out Jane and I had discussed what happened. She told me that Frankie got jumped by 10 girls and she looked horrible. Jane admitted she went to go see her along with Laura. I would probably do the same thing, only I wouldn't want to risk Eric finding out I have friends or even acquaintances. Too much is at risk these days, and I'm not risking my life or anyone else's for that matter.

We've got to make it out of here. And as soon as this journal gives me some insight on where we are, I'll find a way out and free all of the girls who have been trapped here for years now. It won't be long before we've missed our chance to escape, so this has to be done by the end of the year before they let the winner of the drawing go free.

I pull my covers over me and get comfortable. Then, suddenly an alarm went off. I sprang up from my covers, and looked over at Jane who shrugged at me. We heard screaming coming from the hallway. I got out of bed and ran to the door and opened it.

Girls were emerging from their rooms and looking down over the railing. I walked over to the railing and looked down. There on the first floor was a girl lying in a pool of blood. She had jumped. Clyde, Eric, and Luke were holding three girls by their arms. But that's when countless girls soared down the stairs surrounding Clyde, Eric and Luke. They were trying to overthrow them. I smiled in victory and was about to run downstairs myself when Jane stopped me and shook her head and said,

"Don't! They won't make it out the door without the bands off and Clyde has a multi-shock button in his back pocket, once he presses it, all of our bands will shock us." I frowned, but also wondered how she knew that. In an instant a sharp pain seared through my wrist and went through my veins. I fell to the ground, along with every other girl in my sight.

I heard gunshots firing and girls screaming, and I could faintly hear Clyde yelling. A few moments later everything went black.

Chapter 10

My body felt sore as I laid on the cold floor. I blinked my eyes open and saw two girls hovering over me. They gasped and ran away. What the heck? I pushed myself up off the ground and stood to my feet. I looked around, seeing other people standing up, looking confused. The multi-shock must've been pretty bad to give off this effect.

I spotted Jane walking down the stairs and sighed in relief. I'm glad she's okay. Without Jane, I don't think I could have made it through anything. She's like a sister to me, and I really care about her.

I casually walked into the elevator where Jane and the rest were waiting for me, except for Frankie who was still in a lot of pain. The elevator doors closed and that began our meeting. "Anything new in that journal, Sydney?" Jada asked me.

"Well there are some more things that I've discovered, but still no way out." I told them all. Some of them frowned." Have you guys heard about the girl that Eric killed?" I ask them; they all shook their heads.

"Well, Helen is Eric's sister, along with Luke and Kimberly. Eric raped her when he was drunk one night, though he claimed it was an accident. Eric's real name is Arnold, and Luke's real name is

Joseph. Eric got pissed at Kimberly because she called him a rapist and he snapped her neck. Oh yeah, and Eric or Arnold murdered his parents and rebuilt this place with his parents money and is hiding from the police." I rushed out.

Everyone's mouths were hanging open, surprised at finding out all of these secrets. I smiled slightly.

"This is crazy. All along Eric wasn't really Eric, and Helen was lying to us all?" Iris said as she shook her head. This was a lot to take in, I could tell by the looks on their faces.

"Who can we trust?" Laura asked me.

"No one." I answered. "Except each other. Half of these girls would rather turn you in for points then keep a secret."

"Then it's settled. We trust no one, we talk to no one, and we stay away from everyone." Iris declared. I nodded and pressed the 3 on the elevator button panel. I was the first to get off the elevator and head into my room. Jane would be the fourth one off, so it won't be too obvious.

The next morning was rocky. Clyde deprived everyone of breakfast and lunch, so some girls tried to sneak some food from the kitchen. Clyde cut all of their hair off as punishment and told them they weren't allowed to eat dinner either.

People have stopped focusing their attention on me, mainly because there's really nothing they can do about it, so they've just tolerated Eric's favoritism towards me.

Frankie's face was worse than Jane had explained. Her face was swollen and her cheeks were bruised. She had bald patches on her head where girls had yanked out her hair and she was missing a tooth. I felt sorry for her, but all I could do was feel bad for her at a distance. Not being able to comfort my friends was beginning to bug me, and I started to rethink this whole plan we were trying to conjure up, but if we don't leave this place, they'll be in more pain.

I've lost track of the time I've been staying here. Last time I checked, it was two months and a couple of weeks. My family has probably given up on me by now. I wouldn't blame them for doing so, it's hard trying to find someone when you're not sure if their even alive still. I knew Scott would still have hope, he doesn't give up on a lot of things, and since I'm his little sister, I'm pretty sure he wouldn't stop searching for me.

An arm touched my shoulder, making me shiver a bit because I knew it was Eric's. Turning around to face him, I saw he was holding onto someone's hand. And that someone was a little girl. I had seen her around and as far as I know, she's the youngest one here. She smiled up at me, her big

131

blue eyes bursting with happiness. Something told me she didn't know she was in danger, and she had probably forgotten her parents long ago.

"Julia, say hello to my girlfriend, Sydney." Eric told the little girl. I hated how he lied to her, to spare her feelings, but I would do the same. It'd be kind of weird to tell the girl that I was his whore. "Hi, Sydney I'm Julia, it's nice to meet you." I smiled politely and put out my hand for her to shake. She gripped it gently and we shook hands.

"Hi Julia, it's very nice to meet such a pretty girl as yourself." She giggled and mumbled a thank you. I looked up at Eric and he smiled at me, it was kind of awkward so I looked away casually.

"Julia, go downstairs. Sydney and I will meet you there in a second." Julia nodded and walked down the stairs. Eric gripped my arm tightly and pulled me close to him.

"I've decided to take you outside." He whispered into my ear. Instantly I knew this was an opportunity that I couldn't screw up.

"But don't think you can just run away; I brought Julia along in case you get any ideas. If you misbehave, she gets hurt, understood?" He hissed. I gulped and nodded. He released my arm, which was definitely going to be bruised by tomorrow.

There goes my plan of escaping. But maybe this could be a good thing for me. I could scope out the place in search of any possible exits. But I'll have to get out of Eric's sight to do so.

Julia, Eric, and I all stood by the front doors. They were large and bolted shut and could only be open from the control room. The doors slid open with a loud noise. People were all staring at us as we walked out. Many looked envious. I spotted Jane staring at me. She gave me a secret nod and I winked at her. I had to figure out something.

As we stepped out into the sunlight I put my hand above my eyes to see. It had been months since I last saw and felt sunlight. Ever since I've been in here, I've gone pale. The sun on my skin felt nice and warm. Helen had said we were in a forest somewhere, and she was right.

Grass stretched far and wide, and trees surrounded the facility. It was well hidden, which is the reason why no one could find us. Julia skipped through the grass, twirling around with her ponytail swinging from side to side. I touched a strand of my hair, It was dry and breaking. It was longer than it was, but my split ends were terrible. I would kill for hair like Julia's. She was probably treated nicely and given decent shampoo.
Eric glanced back at me and motioned me to come forward. I didn't want to have to stand next to him.

I just wanted to be left alone to gaze at the scenery and not be forced to speak with him.

"So tell me Sydney . . . how are you enjoying my journal, hmm?" I stopped in my place and stared at him. He smirked and continued walking.

How did he know? I had covered my tracks so carefully. Maybe he had searched my room. Or went back to write in his journal and discovered it went missing. He knew...but for how long? Did he know about the elevator meetings?

Maybe he's hoping I'll give up and spill everything. But I won't. I have to stay strong this time.

"It's quite lovely actually. I love how you have that insane psychopathic personality and think you're all innocent and clever." I called out to him, with a small grin on my face. He looked back at me, a little shock visible on his face. He frowned and walked towards me.

"I didn't think you were smart enough to put the pieces together, Sydney. I'm impressed." He grinned.

"Me neither, Arnold." His body froze and his hands clenched. It brought me pleasure to see him get so aggravated with his past.

"Let's keep walking," he murmured and grabbed my wrist. He let it go after we walked in silence for a while.

"You may think you've got me all figured out, Sydney, but you don't." He stopped in his tracks and faced me.

"I did what I did to protect my brother and sisters-"

"So killing your parents was to protect them? And how is raping and murdering your little sister protecting?" I fired back. He raised his hand prepared to hit me, but I didn't flinch. If he was going to hit me, he could, and from the anger I was feeling now, I'd probably hit him back.

His hand dropped down to his side. He then took both of his hands and pushed me to the ground. I yelped, and tried to get up as quickly as I could, but he pinned me.

"You're really pushing it." He growled. His hands went to my collar as he attempted to rip it open, but I fought to push them away.

"I'll scream." I quivered.
"You know what? Since you won't listen, I'll have no choice but to threaten your family." My heart stopped and I looked into Eric's eyes to see if he was serious. And he was.

"Get off me." I commanded him. He rolled his eyes and got off me. I pushed myself up off the grass and walked away in the opposite direction. He always knew how to push my buttons and how to get me upset; threatening my family was one of the things I'd hope he would never do, but he proved me wrong.

I stopped in my tracks for a moment and covered my face with my hands and threw my head back in annoyance.

"Does it satisfy you to bring me pain? You say I'm your favorite, yet you treat me as though I'm a pet rather than the girl you're marrying." I told him. I heard him come up behind me. As much as I hated being his fiancé, I needed to accept the fact that I might not be getting out of here anytime soon.

Maybe after a while, I'd get used to him and his ways…living in the facility and raising my-our child.

Before I could shake the thought, tears began streaming down my face as I started to sob and fell to the ground. My body started to shake as I cried, each thought of staying with Eric forever made me cry harder. I didn't want to live like this. I tried imagining it, but the thoughts were too painful. I didn't want to be married to Eric. I wanted to fall in love with my high school crush and we'd go out, then graduate…go to the same college and afterwards get married and spend the rest of our lives together growing older and older; that was my fantasy. And now that I realize I want something different, my urge to leave this place grew stronger.

"You will never have me." I hissed at him as I turned around to face him. He rolled his eyes and pulled me off of the ground by my arm.

"That's where you're wrong. You will always be mine. All I have to do is threaten someone's life to get you to do what I want." With my head held high, I took my hand and swiftly slapped it across his cheek. He looked a little shocked at first, but that shock turned into anger and he glared down at me.

"I don't love you nor do I like you. You forced me into this. I didn't agree willingly. You will never make me happy and I will make sure my child hates you." I spat. The look on his face showed that I had gotten to him, and that satisfied me. I smirked wickedly and walked away from him, heading back towards Julia who was steadily picking flowers in the grass. She reminded me a little of Maddie; the way she would skip all of the time, or how she always smiled. Part of me wanted to have a child like Julia. I'd like to have a girl, but a boy would be pleasant too.

As I watched Julia play in the grass, I noticed I was smiling. I stopped smiling and turned around, looking away from her. That had been the first time I had truly smiled since Robin and Sarah had died. I told them we'd make it out of here, so I'll make sure that I make it out of here for them.

"Julia come on, it's time to go." Eric walked up from behind me and went to get Julia, who smiled and skipped over to him and grabbed his hand. I sighed and followed behind them. As we headed back to the building, I caught something out of the corner of my eye. Behind a few bushes were gravestones, and I was positive they were for the girls Eric and Clyde had murdered, Robin and Sarah being two of them. So this is where they take the dead bodies; I've always wondered where they went.

Suddenly like a flower, and idea blossomed and I could feel freedom in my grasp.

Chapter 11

"So how did you even end up across the street from your house that night?" Jane asked suddenly.

"It's kind of a long story." I answered, scratching the back of my head. I didn't want to think about the night before or the night of my kidnapping. Both were just too bad to really think about.

"If you're willing to tell it, I'm willing to listen." Jane smiled. I guess I had to then.
"Well…"

My eyes wandered around the buzzing cafeteria. My attention span was as small as a speck of dust and any time I'd see something more interesting, I'd get distracted. I'm going to fail this test; my teacher is going give me a big fat F and I'll be grounded until graduation.

"Hey slut, what's up?" Lisa smirked and plopped herself down next to me, I rolled my eyes ignoring her. Apparently, a rumor had started two days ago about me and some douche on the football team. I knew it was him who started the rumor in the first place all because I refused to go out with him.

"Stop calling me that. It annoys me." I told Lisa who just smiled and shoved her fork into my apple and stole it off of my plate.

"Give it back!" I whined and tried reaching for the apple, but she took a bite of it before I could. "Too slow." she laughed and chewed victoriously.

My fist clenched and I stopped myself from saying something I shouldn't. Stealing my food is one of my pet peeves and I remembered the last time that happened, someone ended up with a fork in their hand, and I ended up with a restraining order. Yeah...it was my aunt. Family reunions are never the same anymore.

Lisa has been my best friend since we were awkward freshmen girls and yet she still steals my food, even though she knows it angers me. But ever since freshman year ended and she became friends with a very popular guy at our school things have changed. Sure, she still hung out with me and stuff, but it was like being popular was more important and at times, she'd leave me all alone, but the girl is like my sister and I wouldn't trade her for anything.

"So you know there's a party this weekend, and you just have to come!" Lisa beamed excitedly, her chocolate strands bouncing up and down as she spoke. I sighed and nodded at her, meaning that I would go. If I hadn't agreed, I would have never heard the end of it. She's somewhat bossy but I love her.

Lisa squealed and hugged me. "This is perfect! Aren't you glad you have an amazing friend like me to invite you to parties? Now all you have to do is convince your parents to let you come over to my house, then we'll head off to the party. It'll be legendary." She rambled on for the rest of lunch about how great the party would be and how drunk she would get, and how many guys she would sleep with. It was tiring to sit there and listen to her, and I was relieved when the bell rang and I had to go off to art class, which was my favorite class of the day.

Walking into the classroom, I immediately spotted Charlie, a good friend of mine. He was also the guy that I've had a crush since the seventh grade, but I've known him since the 5th grade. When he saw me, he motioned me over to sit next to him. I smiled and walked over and sat down.

"Hey Sydney." he said facing me. "Hey, where is everyone?" I asked him, noticing the classroom was rather empty today.

"I'm sure more people are coming. So are you going to Jake's party this weekend? Lisa said you were, but I just wanted to hear it from you." I nodded and he grinned.

"Awesome." Was all he said before the teacher walked in and announced that we were having class outside today. That explains the empty

classroom. We gathered our things and followed our art teacher outside, where everyone was sitting underneath a tree.

Our teacher began the lesson, explaining detail and nature and other artsy things, while I began daydreaming as I stared at the scenery. The breeze blew softly and I looked out to the empty road that connected to our school. A van was parked in the shade of the trees on the side of the road. It looked empty, so I thought nothing of it.

A tap on my shoulder got my attention and I turned around to see everyone staring at me. I blushed profusely and looked up at my teacher. "Miss Crow, my class is not for daydreaming, please pay attention." I nodded and looked back down at my notes while our teacher continued talking.

School ended sooner than I thought and I was already headed towards the parking lot where Lisa and Charlie would be waiting for me. I always gave them a ride to school and back home on Thursday. I still don't understand why, since they both have working cars, but it's become a weekly routine. Not to mention Scott used the car most of the time.

I froze in my tracks and my body stiffened as I watched Lisa aimlessly flirt with Charlie. This was not acceptable. She knows that I like him. Instead *of making a big deal out of it, I walked over and got inside the truck. "Guys come on." I told them. Charlie got in the front and Lisa in the back. As jealous as I was, I didn't bring it up. Lisa would deny it, and Charlie wouldn't say anything at all. After dropping them both off, I headed home.*

When pulling into the driveway, I noticed an unfamiliar car parked in front of my house. Hopping out of the car, I walked up to my front door and walked inside.

"Look who's finally home." A deep voice said. On the couch in the living room sat my brother, Blake. A large smile formed on my face and I rushed over to hug him. He smiled and laughed as I threw my arms around him.

"I had no idea you were coming! Where's Vanessa?" I say. Vanessa appears beside me and we both hug each other, although her enlarged stomach prevented us from hugging normally. "Your stomach has gotten so big! I can't wait to see my little nephew." I chimed. Vanessa smiled softly and nodded. "He'll be just as handsome as his father." Blake rolled his eyes playfully then smiled.

"How long are you guys staying?" I ask them, they both look at each other. "Maybe a few weeks." Blake says. It's obvious they're hiding something, but I guess I could pretend like I don't

notice a thing. They're here now, I don't really care why.

After Scott came home, we all had dinner. We laughed a lot and it felt good to be so happy. Underneath the smiles and laughter, my parents were divorcing, Scott was failing, Maddie was going through a weird phase where she has an interest in blood, and Blake and Vanessa were having financial troubles, which I discovered when I overheard them talking. And I on the other hand was having friendship issues. Lisa was becoming a little more distant and I think it was because of recent rumors about her being friends with the "loser," a.k.a. me. I usually ignore the rumors, but she takes them to heart and I think she's changing.

"You're life seemed pretty rough," Jane interrupted. I chuckled lightly.

"We were far from perfect, but that's what makes us human, right? As much as they annoyed me sometimes, I still loved them dearly and miss them like hell." I told Jane. She gave me a sad smile and patted my shoulder.

"We all miss our families. At least you still remember yours. I've nearly forgotten mine," Jane admitted.

"Really? Do you at least remember their names?" I asked her and she shook her head, "None, except my little brother. His name is Julius. He was two when I left. He should be five years old by now." As she spoke tears rolled steadily down her cheeks and I quickly engulfed her in a hug.

"What ever happened with Lisa and Charlie?" She asked me, switching the subject.

"I'll skip to the night of the party," she nods and I continue, "I had just arrived with Lisa, Charlie had taken a ride from his friend Tommy and they had gotten there before us…"

I looked over at Lisa, who was already getting her flirt on. She knew she looked slutty. I even told her she looked slutty, but that's what she wanted to look like. She wore a short black strapless dress that came up to her thigh and would slide up anytime she'd bent over. I went for something more casual: skinny jeans and a floral shirt.

Inside the house was a crowd of teenagers drinking, dancing, or making out like the typical teenage party. Why had I come here again? My choices have become very idiotic lately, I should leave.
I turned to flee but I bumped into someone. I stumbled back and looked up and saw Charlie. "Sorry about that Sydney," He apologized. I nodded and decided to make my way around him.

145

"Wait. Where are you going?" Charlie grabbed my arm, pulling me slightly back.

"I'm leaving," I stated.

"But you just got here, come on . . . stay." He begged. I sighed a little, "Fine. Just for a few more minutes. I shouldn't even be here." I told him and he smiled.

"What is the loser doing here?" Someone said loudly. Everyone turned around and I saw Taylor standing on a table pointing at me. Taylor always taunted me, but in reality she just had family problems and let her anger out on everyone else.

"I could ask you the same question Taylor," I replied chuckling. Everyone exclaimed and let out a roar of "oohs."

"Ew, get over yourself Sydney. It's not like you're pretty or anything. You don't even have any friends," She retorted.

"Actually I do," I countered. She scoffed and rolled her eyes. "You actually think you have real friends? Lisa and Charlie aren't your friends that's why they're-"

"Taylor!" Charlie barked. I looked at Charlie curiously, then turned back to Taylor," That's why they're what?"

"Dating behind your back," Taylor smirked. I felt my heart skip a beat and I whipped my head around to Charlie.

"Sydney we were going to tell you-"

"Save it Charlie! Because you made the mistake of choosing a slut like Lisa as your girlfriend. She flirts with everything that walks and she dresses like a cheap hooker. She's upstairs cheating on you right now with Bryan from the soccer team." The crowd got so riled up after my little comment and people began to taunt Charlie.

"Dammit. Sydney, can you please let me-"

"No! I'm going to go drag your girlfriend out here on her white ass and beat the crap out of her." I stormed up the stairs, kicking in the door I knew she was in. She was in the middle of a sloppy make out session with Bryan.
"Bryan, I'm going to borrow Lisa for a moment." I told him before pulling Lisa by her arm down the stairs. Many people were watching and cheering and some shocked I had even said those things.

"Sydney, what the hell are you doing? What's going on?" She asked, clueless to what was about to happen.

I tugged her outside on the front lawn and pushed her down. She looked scared and shocked.

"Sydney?"

"You were dating Charlie behind my back." I stated through a clenched jaw. Her eyes widened and she put her hands up in defense, "Sydney, I was going to tell you-"

"Tell me when? After you've slept with him? Lisa, you knew I liked him! I've known you since ninth grade! I've known him since the fifth grade! I flat out told you when we became friends that I liked him! I've liked him since forever and you go and be a stupid slut and start dating him!" I scream at her. By the time I finished, I felt fresh tears streaming down my face.

"I'm sorry." Was all she said.

"Screw you. Don't ever talk to me again." I spat at her and turned to leave. I walked over to her car and opened the door and grabbed my backpack and began walking home. Betrayal was something I wasn't used to, and now that I've felt it, I never want to go through it again.

"After walking home, I had witnessed two girls being kidnapped. I thought the van had left, but they somehow saw me and turned around, almost hitting me. Someone came out and grabbed me and I woke up here," I finished up.

"You mean you were kidnapped after all of that?" Jane gasped.

"Yeah, that day was the worst day of my life. I was going to go home and cry myself to sleep and hopefully get over it the next day, but my future changed when that van turned around," I told her.

"I guess I understand your urgency to get home," Jane muttered and I nodded.

"We should get some sleep, it's late." I suggested. Jane nodded and I flicked the lights off.

If I ever got back home, I was switching schools.

Chapter 12

Something was wrong. Now I wasn't just blabbering like normally, something actually felt off about today and it might've had something to do with me. Jane glanced over at me and raised her eyebrow, I shrugged at her and faced forward and began to focus on what Clyde was saying.

"In a matter of days, we will announce the winner who will be set free." A loud uproar started and girls were squealing and crying and gasping all over the place. This must've been the weird feeling I've been having; the announcement that will change one girl's life. What if it's me?

"Quiet!" Clyde growled and the audience went silent.

"Now, this year, we've received more than seven thousand names in the bucket, which is twice as much as last year. The three contestants with the most names in the bucket are Sydney, Harriet, and Bella." Eyes were glued on me and I felt horrible, but it wasn't like my name being called wasn't expected. Eric had given me so many points for no reason, which was to purposely make my life a lot more difficult here.

"That is all we have to announce today, you are all dismissed." Eric said. Everyone stood and filed out of the auditorium. Eric had motioned me over to him right as I stood to my feet and I walked over to him.

"Yes?"

"Come with me, you have an appointment," He told me and grabbed my hand, holding it in his as we walked. After our talk outside three weeks ago, Eric has kept his hands to himself, except for the occasional hand holding, which I tried to ignore. He had this image in his head that we were an actual couple and that our relationship was normal; or that we were even in a relationship.

We arrived in Helen's office and I sat down on an empty bed. Helen and I hadn't talked since the day she kicked me out of the file closet, we weren't as close as we were, but she's the one to blame. All the secrets she's hidden from me have gotten in the way.

Helen walked over and sat down on the rolling stool. I laid down on my back like I had done numerous times when I came in for these check-ups, only this time I was getting an ultrasound.

"Lift up your shirt," I did as I was told, and Helen took the ultrasound gel and squeezed onto my stomach. She then took the transducer and rubbed it across my belly. She moved it around for a while, staring at the monitor, a black and white picture showing up on the screen where I could see the shape of the child inside me.

"Do you want to know the sex of the child?" Helen asked the two of us.

"Yes," Me and Eric said that in unison. We glanced at each other then turned away awkwardly.

"It's a boy." I smiled joyfully. And was surprised seeing Eric smiling along with me. What bothered me most was that it was his. My child was also his; he'd probably look like Eric, maybe even share some of his habits, but even if my son did share all of those things with Eric, he would never be around to compare them. I was leaving this place, and leaving Eric behind. Eric knew so little about the plan that would take place tomorrow. I wasn't staying here, I wasn't going to rot away and let him corrupt my child with his lies. My chance would come.

"I'll clean this up, and you two can leave." Helen snapped and unplugged the machine. Eric glared

153

at her, but Helen didn't seem to care. She handed me a few baby wipes to clean of the gel then stormed away.

"Sydney, you can head back up to the room, I'm going to talk to Helen for a bit." By talk, he definitely meant yell, but I couldn't do anything about it, so I cleaned myself up and walked out.

I turned down the creepy corridor that was a shortcut to the cafeteria, because I was a pregnant with constant cravings, I got to eat whenever I pleased. I'm trying to keep my weight down, but it was like food was all I wanted nowadays. Right when I turned the corner, I was immediately shoved back against the wall.

"Fancy meeting you here," Luke purred in my ear. I smiled and threw my arms around him, my discomfort towards Luke had faded slightly, and I could actually say that I liked him. I'm wasn't in love; I was far from it, but I could tell Luke was trying to separate himself from his brothers shadow and I'd definitely remember that.

"I've got something for you." He told me, he reached into his pocket and pulled out a tiny photo. My jaw had dropped when I realized which picture it was.

"To Grandma, with love" was written on the back of the picture. I flipped over the photograph and smiled as I looked over the family photo that had been taken years ago. My mom and dad were smiling as mom held my little sister in her arms while Scott and I had our arms around each other, both smiling with missing teeth, we looked goofy yet adorable. Blake stood with his hands in the air, grinning like an idiot. I remembered that was the day my mom got back from the hospital after giving birth to Maddie. Me and Scott were six years old, and Blake was about eleven.

A tear slipped down my face and onto the dusty photo in my fingers. Luke frowned a bit and wiped the single tear away with his thumb.

"I'll see you later Sydney." He said then kissed my forehead; I nodded and kept staring at the picture, going over old memories in my head. I missed them so much, and it only made everything hurt a lot more. It's been months and their eldest daughter is still missing. They've probably forgotten about me-no I shouldn't say that, I'm sure they still haven't forgot about me, but that's no better. I don't want them to waste their time trying to find me. I would get home, I was positive.

"This is Hanna; she'll be helping you deliver your baby when it comes." I smiled at the girl. She looked older than me, but she was much tinnier. Eric smiled at the two of us then walked off.

"Nice to meet you Hanna-"

"You don't have to act like you like me. I'm sure you hate me for what happened so long ago, everyone keeps telling me that you're my replacement, and it's true. I can tell by the way Eric looks at you that you two are in love. I know I can't do anything, not anymore, but I beg you to treat me with respect." she pled. I was utterly confused. What the hell was she talking about?

"Do you mind explaining what the hell you're talking about?" she sighed and leaned against the wall.

"I was Eric's first favorite." I wasn't sure how to react. I thought I had been the only one, yet here she is completely brainwashed and confused saying all of these things.

"Would you tell me everything? I would like to know your story before I question you." she nodded.

"This place wasn't always a prison. Eric had what seemed like good intentions, and I believed in him. Eric had found me on the street, homeless. He took me in and gave me a home. We became very close friends soon after that. We're only a year apart so it's not like his pursues were dangerous, I had a crush on him, and he felt the same." It took me a while to comprehend all this, Eric actually had a heart, apart from the darkness stirring inside of him and the fact that he killed his parents.

"Later on we became official. I was his right-hand girl, and we would always make decisions together. I helped him build this place, at first everyone was free to come and go as they pleased until Clyde came into the picture. Eric said that Clyde was interesting in helping him make this place something great. That he could bring in more money and more runaways, but when Eric let him in, things changed," She started.

"What happened after that?" I asked.

"Rumors started going around that Clyde had forced himself on a girl named Lily, but Clyde denied it and Eric ignored it. Him and Clyde had gotten so close, too close, but I didn't think much about it since I was blinded by my love for Eric. Eric had never hit me nor hurt me in any way. Our relationship turned sexual after a few months, and I got pregnant." Her story was like mine but happier, and lacked the abusive factor.

"Then what?"

"Eric was so excited; he said that he was going to marry me so that we could raise a family together and live happily ever after, just like a fairytale. It was until him and Clyde got too drunk one night and the incident with his sister happened. Only, it wasn't Eric, who had raped her, it was Clyde." I gasped and covered my mouth with my hands.

"In Eric's journal, he was positive that he had raped his own sister!" I exclaimed.

"No, it was Clyde. When Eric passed out drunk, Clyde snuck into Kimberley's room and raped her. He told her to follow his instructions and pretend it was Eric who had done it. She had gone along with it, only because she was afraid of what Clyde would do to her if she snitched. Eric felt terrible, but if I had told him, he wouldn't have believed me, just because he and Clyde were too close."

"How did you find out Clyde had did that to her?" I asked.

"She told me in secret. If Clyde had found out she told me, he would have killed her before Eric had a chance to kill him. It was a mess. That day when Eric snapped his sister's neck, she was pissed at Eric because he was never there for her, and would believe Clyde over his own family. So she told him off, and got killed on the spot. That day, Eric had changed. He wouldn't touch me or come near me, he was afraid he'd hurt me. When I gave birth to my child, he stopped talking to me. He just left me to deal with our child on my own. He's never been the same since then." She finished.

That's when I noticed something familiar about Hanna's face.

"Julia is your daughter? Eric is Julia's father?!" I gasped. Hanna nodded and smiled weakly.

"He treated her so well; I didn't understand how he could kidnap a little girl...but it turns out she's yours." I said.

"I'm grateful that he treats her well, but he stopped letting me see her when she turned three. She doesn't even know I'm her mother," Hanna's eyes swelled up with tears, but she shook them away.

"Eric's coming back, he must suspect something. Listen to me for one second," she looked around her and pulled me to the corner and whispered, "You need to cover your tracks more carefully, some people are starting to notice your little meetings in the elevator and if the wrong people find out, they'll tell Eric. I know you're the one we've all been waiting for. You're going to be our savior Sydney, you're going to be the one to set us all free. Promise me you won't forget about us. Promise me you'll escape and come back for us,"

"I promise." I told her. She smiled then walked away from me just as Eric came through the elevator doors.

He looked back at Hanna then at me curiously but ignored it and grabbed my arm and pulled me to the elevator.

"So, for the cake I was thinking something big…but only two layers…" I mentally blocked out Eric's voice. Did he really want to talk about our stupid wedding cake right now? Was this stupid wedding really his biggest priority? My biggest priority was keeping everyone safe and pulling off this plan perfectly. But from all I heard from Hanna, Eric really did have a soft spot and he was probably taking this less like a victim-attacker relationship and more like we were an average couple.

His delusions were enough for one day and I told him I had a headache and he let me go back to my room.

Jane was waiting for me when I came in.

"Are you sure about this Sydney? What if something happens to your baby?" she fretted.

"We have to go through with this; Eric is talking about wedding cakes Jane, wedding cakes! I can't take another minute of it. Now where are the blankets?" She sighed, giving in and fetched the blankets from her drawer.

"Frankie and Laura also got their hands on some sweaters. Once you put all this on you should wake up with a fever," I grinned at her then hugged her.

"You're the best," she giggled. "I know,"

"Let the fun begin."

Chapter 13

I woke up in a bed of sweat. My body felt stiff and sticky. The room felt like an oven; I swung my legs around and off my bed and attempted to stand, Jane walked in seeing me struggling to get up. She rushed over to me and wrapped her arm around me, supporting most of my weight.

"You look terrible," she said, the corners of her mouth twitching as she held back her grin.

"I didn't think I'd feel this bad. I thought you told me it wasn't that bad." I told Jane.

"It's only going to last for a little while. Now let's hurry up a get you to Helen," she assured me.

We walked into Helen's office and I sat myself down on an empty bed. Jane went off to fetch Helen. I hoped this would all be worth it. Helen came in and put on her stethoscope. She held the back of her hand up to my forehead.

"Seems like a mild fever, but we shouldn't leave it untreated. I'll go get-"

"Wait, Helen," I stopped her.

"Yes?"

"Um...I- are you mad at me?" This was the only thing I could come up with. Plus, it had been on my mind for a while to ask her.

"Why would I be mad at you?" she chuckled.

"You seemed angry the other day when I was here getting an ultrasound."

"Oh...well, if you want the whole and honest truth...then no, I wasn't mad at you. I was mad at Eric for doing this to you. You don't deserve this. You don't deserve any of this. I've prayed and begged and hoped that there'd be some way out of here, but I've lost faith and I constantly have to cope with that and Eric doesn't make it better," Helen's eyes were full of despair. Not once had I actually thought about how she felt about everything that happened to her, but I still couldn't bring myself to trust her.

"I'm so sorry." I whispered to her. Just then I spotted Jane walking out of the storage closet, she gave me a thumb's up and I gave her a quick nod and she left the room.

"Anyways, enough about that, let's get this fever down," she said switching the subject and going to get me some medicine and a cold towel.

The day continued on, slower than I had thought, but it was perfect that way; that way we could execute the plan flawlessly.

"Hey Luke," I greeted him as I walked into the control room.

He turned and smiled at me; he stopped his work and walked over and hugged me.

"So what do you need?" He asked as he released me.

"I just need to talk to you for a moment; this is really important, and I don't want you to say anything until I'm finished." He nodded and sat down as did I.

"I want you to know that I love you, not just as a friend but as a person I care about. I know I've led you on, and I feel terrible about it, but I just want to remain friends, a relationship is too much for me to handle...what I'm really trying to say is that I still want you to be there for me...especially if something bad happens to me, and if it does then I need you to give this note to my parents," I handed him a folded piece of paper. There were mixed emotions spread across his face. He was hurt, and I knew that.

"What do you mean 'if something bad happens to you'?" He repeated.

"I mean exactly that. I just need you to give that note to my parents. It tells them I love them and-"

"Sydney, what the hell are you planning?" he yelled.

"Luke, I don't need you to worry about me." I told him as tears swelled up in my eyes. He looked like he was going to argue back but he just paused and a tear suddenly slipped down his cheek. I couldn't seem him cry, it was already hard enough.

"I'm sorry." I whispered. Looks like I'm going to be saying that a lot today.

"I'll talk to you later Sydney." Luke hurried off and left the control room.

My head was pounding by the time I reached my floor. This was all giving me such a migraine, I

166

don't know if this is going to work or not. If the
plan doesn't follow through, I could get myself
killed-not only myself, but my unborn child also.
My room felt like a freezer and the first thing I did
was slip underneath my blankets, snuggling into
my pillow. Pregnancy causes me to get tired easily,
which most likely will be a possible problem in
the end. I could only hope that we'd make it.
The door opened and in walked Frankie and Laura.
I hopped up and threw a towel over the camera in
the upper corner of the wall.

"What are you guys doing here?" I asked them in
a hushed tone.

"We needed to talk to you." Frankie answered.

"And," I drawled.

"Sydney we don't know about this. Why can't one
of us do it?" Laura suggested.

"Because, I don't want you guys killed! No one
can know that you guys were involved. I'm not
having you guys killed on my watch." I hissed.

"But-"
"No buts. End of conversation, leave my room."

My words were harsh, but they had to know where I was coming from. I caused two of my friends to get murdered because of my stupid idea. I was reckless back then, but now I know better than to let them get involved too much. I won't risk anyone's lives again.

My feet were aching and I really needed some serious rest. Frankie and Laura left the room and I immediately crawled back into bed and fell asleep. *I was outside of the facility, walking barefoot along the grass. With each step I took, the grass behind me would turn brown and lifeless. I found myself frozen in front of a gravestone. It was then that my legs could no longer move as though I was glued to the ground.*

The wind began to blow harder, my hair whipping in my face so I could not see, then moments later it stopped. When I brushed my hair away from my eyes, the gravestone had changed. It no longer had a strangers name engraved on the stone but it had my name. The feeling in my legs returned and I fled from the gravestone.

That's where I ran into a woman with golden hair and stormy grey eyes. She smiled at me and held out her hand. I slowly took her hand and suddenly her face changed and she was now Helen.

"Get away from me!" I shrieked and attempted to remove myself from her grasp.
"Do not fear Sydney, I am not who you think I am," she said to me, her voice as sweet as honey.

"You aren't going to hurt me?" I asked.

"No, and I'm not Helen either. I am the one who you think is your enemy." I was confused by her words and wanted to question her further but she began to fade away.

"My enemy; who is my enemy?" I asked.

"If you do not work with your enemy, you will parish, along with everyone you love,"

"Eric? Why would I work with Eric? He wouldn't help me!" She did not answer, she only continued to fade.

"Please, tell me who it is!" I called out to her but she had already vanished.

I woke up panting heavily. What did this dream mean? Was Helen or whoever that was trying to tell me something? I couldn't decide whether to believe what she said or not, but something told me that that dream was important.

But why would she tell me to work with my enemy? Who is my enemy?
I went through a list of people who I considered my enemy in this place, but it only came down to two names; Eric and Clyde. Although, I'm positive that they're my enemies. Who else could this woman possibly be talking about?

Courtney.

I jumped out of bed and dashed out of the room. By the look of things, it was still early in the day. I glanced up at the clock seeing that it was only four in the afternoon, which meant that the rest of the day, I would spend planning this.

Courtney stayed down on the first floor, which usually belonged to those who had stayed here the longest. I walked over to the bulletin which displayed everyone's schedule. The board was crowded with papers all stapled over each other and I wondered why nobody had sorted this out yet.

"Looking for something?" A familiar voice

questioned.

Without turning around I answered, "Yes, I was actually looking for you Courtney."

"If you've come here to start some drama, I'm not in the mood, especially not for you. Now if you would mind, could you please take you and your slutty ass out of my sight before I shove my foot up your-"

"Geez, can your voice be any more irritating?" I groaned and turned around to face her. She crossed her arms and glared down at me, I never realized how tall she was until now.

"Anyways, I didn't come here to start drama Courtney; I came here to ask for your help." I whispered the last part, just in case there was anyone creeping around.

"My help; you want my help? Wow, you really must be desperate to come to me." She chuckled.

"I'm serious Courtney,"

"What exactly do you want Sydney?" she asked. "Come with me to the elevator. It will be safer if we talk there." I told her.

"Why?" She questioned once again, and before she could annoy me any further, I grabbed her wrist and dragged her to the elevator.

"What the hell?" she yelled as the elevator doors shut.

"I'm planning to escape." I blurted.

"You're crazy, let me off this thing!" She hollered.

"Courtney, why else would I go to you? I don't even like you! But this time, I need us to work together to make this plan work." Courtney calmed down and put her hands over her face.

"Why do you want me to help?" She asked, removing her hands from her face.

"Let's just say that it's a gut feeling. I'm not sure if my plan will work, but with you I'm sure it will, so could we put our issues aside and work together?" I begged.

"You know what…fine. I'll do it. But only because you seem more confident than any of the

172

other girls I've met who've tried to escape this place." She smiled a little bit then got off the elevator on the fifth floor.

Everything seemed to be falling into place. And now Courtney is helping me. This is all so wonderful, but I can tell that something will go wrong; I just don't know what yet.
I was meeting Jane downstairs in our room to start working through the plan. I pressed the elevator button and it went down to three, then I got off.

"Jane?" I whispered as I entered the room.

"It's fine, the cameras are covered and Luke isn't letting anyone in the control room because of *maintenance*." I nodded and sat down on the bed.

"Okay here are the sectral tablets. Only take one for now." She handed me the pill and a glass of water. I popped the pill inside my mouth and drunk it down.

"Now the side effects may get out of control, but it should be enough to trick Eric." Jane smiled.

"What exactly are the side effects?" I asked her, trying to keep my cool, the last thing I wanted was to be throwing up everywhere, I do that already.

"Chest pain, dizziness, drowsiness, unusual bleeding, swelling, hair loss-"

"Hair loss?! Why would you give me something that would make me feel worse than I already am? I can't do this. We can't go through with this plan, it won't work!" I cried out.
"Sydney, stop, it's your hormones talking not you. We're doing this, because I am not staying here another moment. And I was just joking about the hair loss part," I sighed and laid back on my pillow. Jane was right, we've come too far to give up now, and it's better if we try and fail than not try at all.

"Attention girls, there will be a meeting in the auditorium in five minutes. Whoever is late, will face the consequences." A voice came in over the intercom and I could already hear the scuffling of shoes.

"Come on pregnant woman, we've got a meeting to attend." Jane helped me up and we both headed out the door.

In the back of my head I was wondering if this

meeting would be about me, maybe Eric had figured out our plans and was now going to slaughter all my friends just like last time. I shook my head; I couldn't be negative right now, this meeting could be about anything for all I knew.

When we entered the auditorium, I felt my world crumbling down.

Everywhere there were decorations…wedding decorations. The stage was plastered with flower pedals and a long white carpet that trailed down the middle of the isle and almost out the door.

"Surprise!" Eric shouted, appearing on the stage speaking through the mic.

"We're having our wedding today!" He cheered. Jane looked at me with wide eyes, which means she didn't know this was happening either. Some random girl came and pulled me along to behind the curtain. Next thing I knew, they were forcing me into my wedding gown and fixing my hair.

"I need some air." I told them, but it didn't seem like they were listening. "I said I need some air!" I yelled. A few people stepped back, looking at me like I was crazy. The air around me felt hotter and my head felt like it was spinning.

Eric's head popped through the curtain, "Sydney, what are you still doing back here? The wedding is about to start."

"I don't feel very well Eric." I told him truthfully. He looked as though he wasn't buying it and pulled me closer to him and whispered, "You're not getting out of this Sydney."

"I'm not faking this, I really don't feel good. My stomach is cramping! Did you forget that I was pregnant?" I snarled, scaring everyone around me. This was probably the first time that hormones had been beneficial to me.

"Calm down!" He hissed. He pinched the bridge of his nose and pointed to the door.

"If you're feeling any better tomorrow, we'll have the wedding then. Bring Jane with you and make sure that she watches over you."

"Okay I-" All the sudden my body had lurched over and my lunch was all over the floor. Someone rubbed my back and I saw Jane come over and help me up while wiping my mouth with a napkin. Jane helped me over to the door and led me out into the hall.

"You look terrible, I don't think I should've given you those pills," Jane said, worriedly.

"It's too late now; we just have to go through with," I told her. My eyes started to feel heavier and I began to feel drowsy.

"If I pass out, then you have to take over," I told her, slowly feeling my eyes beginning to shut and my legs losing feeling.

Jane's POV

"Got it, but let's at least get you up to your room first." I smiled and walked into the elevator with her resting on my shoulder. As much as I believed in Sydney, I was afraid for her life. She was so brave and strong-willed. All of the obstacles she's overcome, it's amazing that she's still sane. If it were me, I would have given up. I looked up to Sydney; I loved how she came to this place prepared to fight and to escape. I would never forget that.

Once we reached our room, Sydney had already

begun closing her eyes. I sat her down on her bed, pulling back the covers and putting her to sleep.

The sectral is supposed to slow her pulse, to make her appear almost dead. It would only last for a while, so I was hoping that our plan would go smoothly. But now it was my turn to put on the show.

I clouded my thoughts with my family and my brother and how much I missed them. A few tears managed to come out and that was all I needed to convince him.

I reached the auditorium and ran towards him, fake tears streaming down my face. Eric stared at me confused.

"What's wrong?" He asked.

"S-Sydney, she's not breathing!" I told him frantically.

"What?" He shouted and pushed pass me, running for the door. I followed after him as he rushed up the stairs and onto the third floor. He busted through the door and rushed over to her body. .

He put his head on her chest and listened. He then put to fingers to her neck to check her pulse. I'm guessing he couldn't feel it by the painful look etched across his face.

"No...she can't be dead! This isn't possible!" He growled in anger. I took a few steps back, in case he completely exploded.

"Just one more day and everything would have been perfect. I could've had my happily ever after." He muttered his face flushing as he soaked the sheets with his tears.

"This is all just a dream, just a terrible dream!" He yelled and picked up her body in his arms and rocked it back and forth.

"Eric, it's going to be-"

"It's not going to be okay!" He snarled, causing me to flinch.

"I'll make an announcement and we'll have a funeral," I almost let myself panic but I decided to try and change his mind instead.

"No...Sydney wouldn't have wanted a funeral," I told him, although I sounded unsure.

"How would you know? You aren't even her friend,"

"We talk sometimes. We're kind of like acquaintances,"

"To be honest Eric...she didn't like you, nor love you. She was only doing that stuff for her child, that's all she really cared about," I added.

"I know...and no one else really cared about her either, except for Luke and I, a funeral would just be pointless. I should just bury her, and then she could rest peacefully." Eric mumbled sadly.

"Would you help me, Jane?" he asked.

"Sure," I replied.

To be honest, Eric made me nervous. He didn't speak at all as we carried her body outside. He held this blank stare and didn't even start crying again. I've never really talked to Eric much before I met Sydney, he was always busy doing things, and I was never any interest to him or anyone for that matter.

I looked at the sun in the sky and it was almost getting dark. Where was Iris, she's supposed to be out here? I looked towards the main door and watched her tall figure sprint into the woods. I nodded and turned towards Eric.

"Some girl just ran off into the woods!" I told him.

"Which way?" he asked.

"There," I pointed to the direction Iris ran and he took off running, leaving me alone.

"It's time to wake up Sydney." I whispered.

I pulled out the adrenaline injection from my pocket and placed it on the ground as I knelt down and began digging into the dirt that covered most of Sydney's body. I uncovered her face and began clawing at the rest of the dirt that was covering her body. My movements were quick and I was panicking. If the dirt was too heavy, it'd crush the baby, or worse the sectral could slow down her heart rate too much and she'd die.

I managed to move most of the off her and picked up her arm.

"Sydney please be alive," I jabbed the syringe into her arm squeezed the liquid into her bloodstream. I waited a few moments but nothing was happening, but then her eyes shot open and she gasped for air before coughing.

"Thank God Sydney! You need to hurry up; Eric and Clyde have gone after Iris. Frankie and Laura are making sure no one leaves. So you need to go so I can cover up this hole!" I explained, and tried to rush her quickly.

"W-what about Courtney, she's supposed to be out here." Her words surprised me. Sydney had failed to mention that *Courtney* was going to be involved in this.

"When did Courtney join this plan?" I shouted.

"It was last minute, but the plan will fail if we don't have her."

"I'll go get her, stay here." I ordered her.

Running for the door I looked back and saw Sydney standing there, she was counting on me. I arrived at the front door, slipping through the small opening.

"Courtney!" I screamed over the loud commotion coming from the people in the main hall. I saw someone pushing through the crowd, Courtney's face popped up and she ran up to me.

"Sorry I'm late, there are so many people." She told me.

Sydney's POV

I watched as Courtney and Jane ran towards me, that was when I heard two shots go off in the distance.

Courtney and Jane both stopped and looked at each other. I hoped that it wasn't what I thought, that I hadn't gotten Iris killed, but part of me knew that that's what probably happened.

"Come on, now! We need to go! Jane head back to the facility!" I commanded her.

"Sydney?" Someone yelled. Clyde and Eric walked out from the woods.

"Jane, Courtney, run!" I yelled. Everything began to move quickly as we dashed through the woods. I stumbled over branches, my feet aching below me. Twigs snapped and leaves crunched, I could hear their voices yelling behind me, but I didn't care, I was getting away, no matter what. I jumped over logs, weaved through the trees; the scenery sweeping past me.

My body felt weak and if I gave up for even a second, I'd go tumbling to the ground. Luckily the adrenaline was working, pushing my body to go faster.

183

I didn't stop to see the others; I just hoped that they were okay and running as fast as I was. I couldn't tell where I was headed, but I knew that they were catching up.

"Sydney!" Someone screamed. My body was tackled to the floor the moment a gun went off. The person on top of me screamed, and I realized that it was Courtney…she had been shot.

"Oh no," I wept, crawling from under her. I leaned over her body and saw that she had been shot in her abdomen which was steadily bleeding.

"Sydney go, I'll be fine; this was why I was here, right?" She coughed, blood sputtering from her lips.

"If you run, I'll just kill her," Clyde said as he walked up, cocking his gun.

"You wish." Jane aimed and fired at Clyde, the bullet striking his chest, he fell to the ground with a thump. Eric had caught up, his eyes full of anger. I wonder where she got the gun from. I noticed the familiar design and realized it was the gun that Clyde had used to kill Robin and Sarah.

"Sydney, please don't do this. I need you." Eric begged.

184

"I don't want you, can't you see that? You need to let me go. I will never be yours, Arnold," My words were laced with confidence; it was something that I was happy to finally say. Eric hesitated, his eyes narrowing but then softening.

"Then go, before I change my mind." He said. And it surprised me, but I didn't question it, I just turned back to Courtney and Jane.

"Jane, help me with Courtney," Jane and I held Courtney up by putting her arms around our shoulders; she was limping as we walked towards the outlet of the forest. Every part of my body ached and in a couple of moments I felt as though I might pass out.

"I can't walk anymore," I winced as I fell to my knees, bringing Jane and Courtney down with me.

"You two stay here I'm going to try to find a ride!" Jane took off in a sprint along the dirt road. I looked down at Courtney who looked like she was barely holding on.

"We're going to make it out of here Courtney, I promise." I whispered to her as I pulled her so she could rest her head on my lap. My body was shaking and I couldn't help but start to sob.

"S-Sydney?" Courtney stammered.

"Yes?"

"I'm sorry,"

"Don't worry about it, you've helped me escape, I don't need an apology," She nodded slightly.

"Oh a-and Sydney?"

"Yes?"

"Could I-I ask you a f-favor?"

"Anything, ask anything," I whispered.

"Would you name y-your b-baby after my little brother C-Caleph? I know I-I probably don't deserve it but…I just thought it was a pretty good name,"

"I will, I promise," I told her wiping the tears from my eyes. She gave me a faint smile then slowly closed her eyes.

"Courtney?"

"Courtney wake up; oh God! Please, please, please no!" I wept and screamed, feeling my world being swallowed by sorrow. The pain was unimaginable, I didn't want anyone to die, and everyone was supposed to be fine! But maybe this was just so I could make it out and set all of the other girls free. I didn't have time to feel guilty, I had to get to safety.

I stood up, leaving Courtney's body where it was and walked out onto the dirt road. The fresh air smelt wonderful, and once I got back home, I was never staying inside again.

In the distance, I saw a red truck coming down the road, as it neared it began to slow down and that's when I saw Jane on the passenger side.

"Get in we're taking you and Courtney to the hospital." I sighed and shook my head, Jane clamped a hand over her mouth and a few tears slipped from her eyes.

"But we can't just leave her there!"

"She'll be fine." I assured her. Jane nodded and helped me up into the truck. We started down the dirt road, the wind filling up the car and brushing my hair. I pressed my hand against my stomach and felt a small movement from inside and then another.

"He's kicking the babies kicking!" I squealed in excitement. I was happy to realize that the baby was perfectly fine. Jane put her hand on my stomach and gave me a bright smile.

"Something good comes out of everything." She told me and she was right.

Three months later…

"Tell me Sydney, what was it like being there?"

"It was chaos, like being trapped in a box with two hundred other people. Things get crowded and a little overbearing," I responded.

"Now is it true that you were sexually assaulted and got impregnated by your captor?"

"Yes it's true. I was almost five months pregnant when I escaped." I answered.

"Do you think you'll ever get over the things you went through?" The reporter asked. I paused thinking over the question for a little bit.

"I don't think anyone would, especially when your son looks exactly like the man who kidnapped and abused you. When you experience something like what I went through, it's impossible to forget.

188

There were so many terrible things that happened to me and the other girl's that lived there. But at the same time it's something I've escaped and I'm proud of that,"

"Yes," the reporter nodded.

"Now onto my final question: how did you figure a way out? When the police and investigators searched the building, they mentioned the amazing security system."

"Red bull helped me a lot," The audience laughed along with the female reporter.

"No, I'm joking, but I guess it was just my will to go free. I needed to escape, I needed to see my family again and I wasn't going to let anyone stop me. Determination was how I survived. I also promised someone that I would escape and come back for them…and I did."

"Well that's all the time we have, it was great to have you Sydney." I shook hands with the reporter, giving her and the cameras a smile. I exited the stage and went behind the set, meeting my family.

These constant interviews had been going on for month and all I really wanted was a break and some time to spend with my family. Everyone hugged me all together in a warm group hug.

"Are you ready?" my father asked me.

"Yes." I smiled. I was finally going home. I had been staying in a hotel for months because I couldn't quite bring myself to go back there just yet.

The drive home felt long and I was anxious to see my old neighborhood again. Nothing was going to happen to me, I was going to be safe at home with my family and child. The car pulled into the driveway and I glanced at Scott who was smiling at me.

"It's going to be fine." He assured me. I nodded and took a deep breath before opening the door and stepping outside into the autumn air. I pulled my jacket tighter around me and began to walk towards the front door.

Scott wrapped his arm around my shoulder as we walked. He could be such a great brother sometimes, I've really missed him.

Mom unlocked the front door and let us all in. It felt weird being inside my home; everything looked and smelled the same. We still had the same old furniture; nothing had changed like I hoped it would. I had hoped they had gone on without me so that way I wouldn't be reminded of how things used to be.

"You guys could have at least got a new paint job." I joked. Mom and dad laughed.

"The paint was the last thing on our minds."

"I'm fine; you guys don't have to treat me like I'm some expensive face that you're too afraid to break so you don't bother touching it."

"You're right. Welcome home sweetheart, you can go upstairs and freshen up, dinner will be ready soon." Mom kissed my forehead then went into the kitchen with dad.

"Scott, where's Caleph?"

"He's with Vanessa, Blake and Carly, they all went to the store." I nodded and continued up the steps.

My room hadn't been changed, except for the curtains which were now a dark red. I trailed my fingers along the bedspread then over my nightstand. I noticed a familiar journal that sat on top of my dresser. I opened it and flipped through it, stopping on the last page.

191

I just wish that I could go away! My family is breaking apart and Lisa seems like she's drifting away. It's like no one is here for me. Why can't someone just take me away from this home and this town! I just want to escape.

By the end of the paragraph I had tears in my eyes. Looks like my wish came true; this was probably some cruel punishment that I deserved for being ungrateful.

I walked over to the curtains and opened them. My heart stopped when I saw a piece of paper tape to the window. I was almost too afraid to read it, but I did.

This isn't over. You are mine and will always be mine Sydney Crow. And what belongs to you belongs to me. You should be a little more careful about who you let watch OUR child. Little Caleph is getting so big. I hope you don't mind me watching after him for a while.

Love always, ERIC (Arnold)

My heart began to beat faster before my hands hit the window as I let out agonizing screams, the glass shattered and I fell to the floor, my hands clenched into a fist. I pounded on the floor, blood soaking the clean carpet; I heard footsteps rushing up the stairs. I snapped, throwing things from my dresser to the floor.

"Sydney calm down!" My father yelled.

"He's going to kill me!" I screamed, the pain in my chest getting more and more unbearable.

Scott pulled me into his chest and tried hushing my constant screams that I couldn't help but let out. My world was crumbling.

"Call 911, now!" My mother yelled. I pushed Scott away from me, standing to my feet, trying to run away. I couldn't feel the air around me, I could feel my throat closing and my legs weakened and I fell to the floor, the sounds around me became one jumbled mess. Everything went numb and all I could do was lay there trying to comprehend my reality. This was real and there was nothing I could do about it this time.

To be continued...

ACKNOWLEDGEMENTS

I want to acknowledge my cousin and best friend Akane Barnett for her love and support. I also want to thank all of my family members.

I want to offer a special thank you to my WattPad followers.

Last but not least, I want to thank God for helping me along the way.